Wed, Dead and Gingerbread

A Slice of Life Cozy Mystery, Volume 2

Rachel Beattie

Published by Rachel Beattie, 2024.

WED, DEAD AND GINGERBREAD

First edition. December 6, 2024.

Copyright © 2024 Rachel Beattie.

ISBN: 979-8224341115

Written by Rachel Beattie.

Chapter One

"She's dead to me! Do me a favor, ok? Don't mention the name *Bella Villodan* again until after the wedding."

The Slice of Life diner is quiet this morning, which means Anna Chambers's high-pitched screech carries. I don't remember the diner looking quite so festive last time I was here at Christmas, and I wonder if I have Anna to thank for the picture-perfect decorations, even if she may also be the reason for the distinct lack of customers we have right now. I smile wryly at the gaudy sprig of mistletoe hanging directly over the door and decide that this must be one thing Matt, and not his fiancée, is responsible for. He always joked that his favorite thing about Christmas was using mistletoe as an excuse to kiss all the girls he wanted. *Well, that won't last for long, once Anna has that ring on his finger.*

I risk a glance at the one table in the whole diner that's occupied and my heart sinks. Once this wedding goes ahead, there's a lot about Matt that's going to have to change. I wonder how much of my friend will be left after he finally becomes *Mr. Anna Chambers.*

"Veronica!"

I jump, wondering if she's somehow read my mind. While Anna's holed up here on important wedding-planning business, it's like nothing and nobody else matters. Not Matt, who's somehow escaped this particular meeting, not Caroline Mackie, the second of Anna's most devoted friends, and certainly not me.

"Veronica! Coffee!" She actually clicks her fingers and I stifle a groan, reminding myself that the only reason I have this job is because Matt Taylor was generous enough to find me a few casual shifts right when I needed them. Although, judging from just how often he's been away from work lately, I reckon he needs me just as much as I need him. I take a deep breath and pour two cups of sweet, gingerbread-flavored coffee. I hesitate over the syrup then opt for a sugar-free alternative, counting silently in my head as I make Anna's coffee to the careful specifications she laid down earlier that morning. My former high-school nemesis is nothing if not exacting, and I know she won't hesitate to complain to Matt if she thinks it'll get me in trouble with my new temporary boss.

"Coming right up!" I call, perfecting my cheery sing-song voice as I carry both cups over to the small table in one corner of the diner that Anna has claimed as her own since before the diner even opened up this morning. "Two gingerbread lattes."

Caroline, Anna's best friend and personal secretary, smiles and accepts one of the cups but freezes before taking her first sip when she hears Anna's sharp voice.

"Did you follow my instructions? Freshly ground single-origin coffee? Heated milk precisely to temperature? Sugar-free syrup?"

"I made it exactly the way Matt showed me," I say, with a prim smile. "And I'm sure you have him perfectly trained by now."

Anna's eyes narrow and I know she's trying to find an insult in my words, but I learned from the expert. *You.* I hold her gaze and widen my smile just a fraction.

"Of course, if you aren't satisfied I'd be more than happy to make you a fresh cup."

She takes a slow sip of her coffee and I sense Caroline is holding her breath until her friend gives a verdict. I know I am. Anna relishes her moment of supreme power, but even she can't resist a contented sigh as she places her cup down on the table and turns back to the pile of papers in front of her.

"It'll do."

It isn't a thank you, but it's about as close as I'm going to get and I accept it with all the grace I can, swallowing my annoyance until I see Caroline offering me a silent smile of gratitude before taking a sip of her own drink. It startles me, this show of almost-solidarity, and for a moment I stay rooted to the spot until my presence draws Anna's irritated attention for the second time in two minutes.

"Did you want something else?" She flips a page in her planner before lifting her head. "In case you hadn't noticed, we are quite busy."

"Right. Of course." I hurry away, swallowing what I'd really like to say to the Wicked Witch of Westhaven. If my job wasn't on the line I'd like to give her a real piece of my mind. But then I remember the request Matt made of me when we last talked about his choice of girlfriend. *I wish you two could get on. Can't you at least try, for my sake?* Taking a deep breath, I grab a plate and pile it high with freshly frosted gingerbread cookies, then return to Anna and Caroline's table. I plonk the plate down without much ceremony and force myself to smile. "I thought you might like something sweet to help you along. Wedding planning must be tough, especially so close to Christmas."

"It would be a lot easier if my maid of honor hadn't just left town." Anna makes a careful note in the middle of an incredibly detailed list, then reaches for a cookie. She chews absent-mindedly, and it falls to Caroline to act as interpreter. She's never been one to avoid talking, even to me, and as she takes a pretty piece of gingerbread she turns in her chair to face me a little more directly.

"Bella won a place on a cruise to the Bahamas, can you believe it?" Bella Villodan is the third corner in their triangle of meanness and I decide her absence certainly won't make this Christmas a less pleasant experience. If it makes Anna's life a little more difficult that's a bonus. My gaze strays to the large glass windows that face out onto the snowy Westhaven high street and I shiver, despite the relative warmth of the diner.

"It's nice for some!" My laughter stops short when Anna lifts her head to glare at me.

"I still think she might have stayed in town for Christmas. I know she's desperate to escape everything that happened recently but she was supposed to be my maid of honor. She has responsibilities. And she's my best friend. What kind of best friend would choose a cruise over my wedding?"

I resist the urge to look at Caroline, who hesitates just a moment too long before jumping in with a few soothing words.

"Well, you know I'm going to help as much as I can. And I'm sure Veronica..."

"Oh, it looks like I finally have another customer!" I hurry back to the counter before I accidentally get myself roped into helping at a wedding I resent even happening. I promised Matt I'd try and respect his choices: that doesn't mean I have to climb aboard the bridesmaid train, even if Anna did get desperate enough to ask me. She's never liked me and has hardly been head of the welcome team since I came back to town a few months ago, so I expect I'll fall somewhere near the bottom of her list of people to ask for help. That doesn't mean I want to offer it.

The door to the diner swings open and I fix a warm, welcoming smile on my face, hoping that this is just the first of many festive visitors we'll get today. *Anything that dilutes the Anna Chambers effect will be a good thing, especially if it's likely to boost our takings.* I know even the busiest times of the year have lulls, but this is getting a little ridiculous and I don't want Matt to blame me when his profits are down.

"Happy Holidays! What can I get you -"

I'm startled to realize I don't recognize my new customer - an oddity in itself in a town where just about everyone knows everyone else. The last new arrival was me, and considering I grew up here, that doesn't exactly count.

"Is it always so cold around here?" The pretty stranger lets out a musical laugh, then begins to unwind a comically long woolen scarf from around her slim neck. "I guess it's about time I came into town to heat things up a little!"

"Amy?"

"In the goose-flesh!" The young woman shrugs out of a huge parka to reveal a slim, scantily-clad body and waves a delicate hand in my direction. "Turn the heat up a little, can't you?" She straightens an intricate gold locket, smooths her chestnut curls, and turns back to Anna, who is staring at her as if she's just seen a ghost. "Well, don't just sit there, Anna-Banana! Come and give your best friend a hug!"

· · · ·

"SO, HAVE YOU EVER MET this *best friend* before?"

By the time Matt makes an appearance at the diner his fiancée has all but abandoned her oh-so-important wedding prep and is instead engaged in an excited - and loud - game of *I remember when* with her newly arrived in town oldest best friend. Amy Callaghan might be a stranger to me and to just about everyone else in Westhaven, but she certainly isn't a stranger to Anna.

"I can't believe you are still wearing that necklace!" Anna laughs as Amy strikes a pose, displaying the locket that I now see is not only intricate but old.

"Of course I'm still wearing it!" Amy pulls her friend into a hug. "My best friend gave it to me!"

Their display of friendship might be endearing if it wasn't quite so loud.

"Which best friend?" Matt is watching Anna's table almost as closely as I am. And I notice that her cozy twosome has become a decidedly less cozy trio. Ever since Amy burst through the doors of the diner, she's captured all of Anna's attention and affection, and neither of them seems to remember Caroline is even there. I see her shift her chair a little closer to Anna so that she ends up almost sitting on her friend's lap and feel a flash of unexpected sympathy as one glare makes her move it away again.

"I always thought Anna and Bella were the platonic power couple of Westhaven," I say, reaching past Matt for a bottle of spray-cleaner and a cloth. "But I wonder if I overlooked poor Caroline's degree of devotion. It's quite sweet really. Or it would be if her object of admiration wasn't...you know..."

I don't mean to share my thoughts out loud like this, I really don't, and as soon as I see the dark shadow settle over Matt's face, I regret it. I smile and offer a swift apology which doesn't seem to be particularly convincing. He continues to frown at me, and I squirt a little cleaning spray at him which makes him splutter and back away from me.

"You realize that stuff is toxic, right?"

"Wrong." I spritz the air again, then lean forward and take a big breath in. "Mmm, mulled cider."

Matt gives me a dubious look, then sniffs the air. His frown shifts almost imperceptibly to a look of mild - but affectionate - resignation.

"What did you do?"

"I just made one teeny, tiny change to the way things run around here." My heart beats a little quicker and I find myself stumbling over my words in my eagerness to share them. "I bought some new cleaning supplies from Melissa Barnes. She's launching a whole new range in time for Christmas. All natural, organic, locally sourced...and they smell really, really good." I spritz the air again and take a noisy inhale. "See?"

"And she just gave you a bunch of free samples?"

"Not entirely...but they were very heavily discounted." I feel my cheeks warm under Matt's scrutiny. "And it's not like a few pennies here and there is going to make much difference to you. Not when you run such a successful business. I mean, the Slice of Life diner is prime Westhaven real estate, especially at this time of year." I glance around the diner, glad that it's filled up with regulars in the last hour or so, otherwise my argument wouldn't be quite so convincing. "Look at all these customers! Your profits make a profit! Melissa's just getting started out. She needed a little boost."

"Alright, alright." Matt holds his hands up, palms out to ward off the rest of my over-eager justifications. "Just remember I hired you to work here in a casual capacity, alright? I'm not looking to take on a new business partner. Not even one who knows this place almost as well as I do." He reaches into the pocket of his apron, then pats down the back pockets of his jeans, before scanning the area, looking for something. I swiftly reach into a small drawer underneath the cash register which had been a repository for dust and old receipts until just today, when I repurposed it as a handy-dandy device safe. I pull out Matt's phone and hand it to him.

"I think you'll find I know this place *better* than you do, especially lately." His phone blasts an alarm that kicks in the second he takes it from me and he has just enough time to rearrange his features into a smile before Anna hears the alarm and immediately leaps into action.

"Is it time for us to go, babe? Yes, oh my goodness, I can't believe I almost forgot! Amy, I'm going to have to leave you here for a half-hour or so. Important wedding business!" Her eyes sparkle as she looks at Matt and I'm surprised to see the loved-up smile my old friend wears as he walks towards his soon-to-be wife.

"I'll stay here too, shall I?" I call after him, choosing not to point out that my casual shift ought to have ended an hour ago. "Just don't be gone too long. Remember I said I had to be out of here by five." Matt acknowledges me with a wave and holds his other hand out to Anna, who takes it in both of hers. They pause in the doorway to kiss under the mistletoe and I notice Caroline look away from their nauseating show of affection. Only, it isn't exactly nauseating. It's almost...sweet.

It must be the magic of Christmas. That's all. Christmas and a wedding is textbook romance, even when the couple is the least likely match in all of town!

I return to my cleaning with a vengeance and think that Melissa had better continue to give Matt the discount she offered me to switch to her all-organic, all-locally-sourced, all-magic cleaning supplies, or else risk losing her first customer before she even properly launches her new product line. I'm grateful to him for giving me some work over Christmas, wedding or no wedding, but I know that sooner or later I'm going to have to branch out and find a job of my own. I just can't imagine what that would be. It's not like I left my life's calling behind me, but being back in Westhaven means my options are decidedly limited, and if I don't want to end up with casual work for the rest of my life I'm going to have to come up with some kind of alternative. *Maybe I can model myself after Melissa and become an entrepreneur.* I remember my few failed attempts at crafting anything worthy of sale and grimace. *Then again, maybe not...*

"Hi, Veronica."

My head snaps up at the subdued greeting and I'm more surprised than ever to hear it coming from perpetually-chipper Caroline Mackie.

"What are you doing?" she asks, her gaze bouncing off me to stare morosely out of the window after the departing figures of Matt and Anna.

"Cleaning." I pointedly scrub at a spot, then count the job done. "What can I get for you? Another coffee?" I'm already halfway to the machine when Caroline sighs.

"No, thank you." She looks lost without Anna there to direct her, and I'm about to ask about Amy when an obnoxious, tinny ringtone makes her jump out of her chair.

"I have to take this." She waves dismissively towards Caroline and me. "Tell Anna I'll be right back, won't you, Cora?"

I open my mouth to correct her but Caroline looks like she's about to cry. I've been on the outside of friendship circles enough to recognize that feeling, and I switch my focus, offering her a companionable smile.

"How about tea instead? We have this amazing spiced orange and ginger flavor that Matt has stocked especially for the festive season." I reach for two clean cups and jangle them towards her with a grin. "I'm due a break about now anyway. Keep me company?"

Caroline smiles, and not for the first time I remember why I always thought of her as the nice one of her mean-girl group. She's pretty harmless, really, and it's been a while since I had a girlfriend to gossip with over some tea - both literal and figurative.

"Break out a couple more of those gingerbread cookies," Caroline says, as the door to the diner swings closed behind Amy, "and you've got yourself a deal."

Chapter Two

I'm just turning the key in the front door when I hear a terrifying thud from inside my house and I hurry inside, already panicking that the sound I heard was my dad collapsing to the ground and undoing all the good progress he's made in recovering his health over the last few weeks.

"Hey, Ronnie!"

I needn't have worried. Dad is standing perfectly capably on his own two feet and my heart rate slowly returns to normal until I notice the chaos that surrounds him. I pick my way carefully across the room and look at the pile of picture frames, school trophies, and other mementos from my childhood that are now heaped in an untidy pile on the floor.

"Just doing a little bit of reorganizing." Dad stoops to pick up the things he dropped but I shoo him away, practically forcing him back into his favorite easy chair before I turn to address the mess.

"You were supposed to be resting," I remind him, angling one frame so I can see what picture it contains, then wish I hadn't. I grimace and promptly bury my old prom photo in the middle of the pile. "Where did you even find all this stuff?"

"In your room." He props his feet up on a stool and looks hurt when I glare at him. "What? I wasn't rummaging in your business. I just wanted to get some of your old things out on display. This is your home again too now, after all. Don't you want it to feel like you live here?"

"I do feel like I live here," I say, trying to see this as the nice gesture Dad meant it to be. "Or else I wouldn't be wasting my time cleaning the bathrooms and making sure the trash gets collected on time." I pick up a trophy and turn towards my dad with a look of disbelief. "And what makes you think I want to see a trophy I won for a spelling bee when I was seven? That was over twenty years ago!"

"Was it? That can't be right." Dad fusses for the pair of glasses he refuses to wear, even though he can hardly see three feet in front of him without them. "Well, maybe that can stay in storage, then. But the rest..."

"The rest can stay in storage too!" I protest, hastily tossing things back into an empty box. "That's where it belongs. Or, better yet, throw it out altogether. If you're desperate for me to add my personal touch to the place I have a cute candle holder I bought from Melissa that I can bring down to put on the mantel." I glare at him. "Happy?"

"Yes." Dad nods, then his smile drops. "Wait, you say this is a *cute* candle holder. Cute how?"

"It's fine, Dad. I promise there's nothing pink and sparkly about it. It's perfectly display-worthy."

Dad mutters something that sounds suspiciously like *that's what I'm afraid of* but obediently smiles at me as I file the last piece of my childhood back in the box it came out of and shove it hastily under the coffee table out of reach.

"So how was your day?" I ask, retracing my steps back towards the door so I can kick off my boots and shrug off at least two of my outer layers. There's a pile of mail sitting near the front door and I reach for it, instinctively flipping through it for anything that looks like it might be a bill. After spending the last few weeks getting my father's financial house back in order I'm on high-alert for anything that might have gone unnoticed. So far, though, it looks like nothing more than a collection of holiday cards. I split the pile in two and head back into the living room, passing one half to Dad as I slide past him and drop heavily onto the sofa.

"How was *your* day? Was the diner busy?" Dad opens the first of his envelopes and flips open the card, rolling his eyes at the cloying sentimentality. He lifts his gaze, watching me a little more intently than I realize at first. "You look tired."

"I'm fine," I reassure him, smirking at one of our neighbor's *festive funnies* cards, then offer it to Dad. "Here, you might like this one a little better. From Peter Hague."

"Aunt Marjorie," Dad says, referring to the artistic snow globe scene he passes my way. "In full festive flow."

Intrigued, I flip the card open and feel my eyebrows lift. Aunt Marjorie hasn't just signed our card, she's covered it in elegant red and green script.

"Is this a poem?"

"Certainly appears to be." Dad chuckles at Peter's card and props it up near his chair so he can look at it again at his leisure. "I hope she isn't expecting anything like that in return." He eyes me. "If she does, that's on you. I am a strictly signatures-only kind of guy."

"And when have you ever sent holiday cards to anyone, signed or not?" I ask, filing Aunt Marjorie's name and address away in my brain for future attention. Christmas is getting pretty close and *sending holiday cards* is so far down the list of jobs I need to get done that it's in danger of being forgotten altogether. "Maybe we can write some together tonight," I suggest. "I think I found a box languishing away with the rest of our holiday decorations."

Dad frowns at the forlorn-looking tinsel I tucked around a few picture frames on the wall and I hurry to offer an alternative.

"Or we can buy some new ones tomorrow. Maybe you can do some of your resting and recuperating at the diner, then we can write them while I'm at work."

"You're working there again tomorrow?" Dad's frown shifts from our sorry-looking Christmas decorations to me. "I thought this was just a casual thing."

"It was." I tug at a loose thread on my sweater. "It is. But it's not like I don't need the money. And Matt needs all the help he can get at the moment. He's so busy with wedding preparations."

"Ah."

That single word is loaded with all the experience that being a girl-dad of twenty-plus years has afforded Edgar Swan and I draw a quick breath in before fixing a smile on my face and acting with an ease I don't feel.

"There was a bit of excitement on that front this morning. It seems poor Anna was in danger of being a bridesmaid down. Bella Villodan skipped town." I see Dad's eyebrows rise and fight a laugh. "Unfortunately, she'll be back again in a couple of weeks. She won a ticket for a cruise to the Bahamas, can you believe it?"

"At Christmas?"

"There are worse places to spend a week," I say, pointedly eyeing the thermostat which I have turned down to a frugal - if chilly - 68°F. "Anyway, Anna is taking it as a personal slight that her friend would rather spend a week in the sunshine than be stuck here in Westhaven being a bridesmaid, so we all got to hear about it." I wince. "Matt suggested me as a replacement, but for some reason, Anna didn't go for that."

Dad snorts and I grin.

"Anyway, it all seems to have worked out, because she had an old friend roll into town right on time to take Bella's place. Amy...something?" I hesitate. "Callaghan. Amy Callaghan. Do you remember her? Apparently, she and Anna go way, way back but I've never heard of her before."

"Which is in itself shocking, considering just how many confidences you've shared with Anna Chambers over the years."

I toss a scrunched-up envelope at Dad but am forced to acknowledge his words. Anna and I were frenemies in school, and we've remained so ever since I came back to town. The little I know about her life - courtesy of her link to Matt - is already more than I ever wanted to know.

"Well, it's good timing anyway. Anna gets her replacement bridesmaid and Amy is keen to hang on her every word and shower her with compliments."

"Everyone's happy, then." Dad resumes opening the rest of the holiday cards I handed him and apart from the occasional chuckle the room falls silent. Dad's words play over in my mind, and I can't quite shake the image I had of Caroline Mackie looking miserable as her friend ditched her in favor of someone new.

It's funny. I never thought I'd find it in me to feel sorry for one of those three. But Caroline was never quite as out and out mean as Anna and Bella, even back in high school. And I guess even mean girls deserve to be happy at Christmas...

• • • •

I'M JUST ABOUT TO START prepping for dinner when there's a knock at the door and I am halfway down the hall to answer it when I hear my dad start huffing and puffing to get out of his chair.

"Don't strain yourself!" I call, hearing him sigh contentedly, and settle back into his seat. I roll my eyes, pretty sure that all that noisy effort was all for effect. No matter how much Dad complains about his slow recovery, there's a lot he likes about being waited on hand and foot. Like leaving me to deal with unexpected visitors on a Tuesday night. Whoever is waiting for an answer is eager, and there's another nervous knock before I manage to pull the door open and jump backward in surprise at who's standing on the other side of it.

"Caroline?"

"Here." She shoves a heavy casserole dish into my hands and I'm so surprised I almost drop it, before getting a better hold. "My aunt asked me to drop this in for you." She's shivering, and without a dish to hold onto, she wraps her thin arms around herself, stamping her feet against the cold.

"Come in," I say, as much to save myself from the frigid night air as my unexpected caller, and I take a hasty step back, welcoming her over the threshold and closing the door behind her. "Who asked you to bring us this?"

"My aunt." Caroline pulls off her woolly hat and fusses with her hair, which looks as perfect as ever. A cascade of golden curls bounces over her shoulders Her gaze meets mine with a flash of surprise that I don't immediately know who she's talking about. "Pamela Kaufman?"

"Pamela Kaufman is your aunt?" I realize I did have this fact buried somewhere in my subconscious and cover my forgetfulness with a smile. "Of course Pamela Kaufman is your aunt. You even look a little alike!" Caroline's features drop into a frown and I decide I've made another faux pas as far as she is concerned. "Well, not very much alike. Not at all. Look, let me go put this down." I heave the casserole dish into a better grip. "It's heavy!"

"It's lamb casserole," Caroline says, as if that explains things. She tiptoes after me, looking curiously around the hallway and I realize this is probably - no, definitely - the first time any of my high school nemeses have ever been in my house. *I guess it's fitting that the first guest is the historically least awful of the three.*

"Can I get you something to drink?" I ease the casserole dish onto the counter and lift up the lid, catching a glimpse of the delicious-looking stew. "Or something to eat?"

"Why don't you ask your friend if she wants to stay and join us for dinner?"

I jump and both Caroline and I whip our heads around in unison, startled to see that Dad has shuffled into the kitchen after us. He grins and then offers her his hand.

"Good evening, Ms. Mackie. Good of you to bring over our dinner right on time. It'll save Ronnie cooking." He winks. "And it'll save me from eating Ronnie's cooking."

"Hey!"

I'm mildly offended, but Caroline smiles and I see my father wilt just a little. I guess he sees more than a passing resemblance between Caroline and her aunt, too. I'm still not completely at ease with the budding friendship he has with

Pamela Kaufman, especially not now that I recall this particular family connection, but if it means we keep getting brought meals like this one I suppose I can learn to live with the situation.

"You'll stay for dinner, then?" He glances past Caroline at me. "Put the stove on, Ronnie. Let's heat this baby up. The casserole." He clarifies, with a chuckle that is apparently contagious, because it makes Caroline laugh too.

"Do you know, I think I will stay if you're sure you don't mind?" Caroline glances at me, looking momentarily anxious and I remember that same fleeting discomfort I noticed in her at the diner earlier today.

"Of course not." I smile and point towards the dining table. "Take a seat. I'll fix us some drinks and get this warmed through."

I can hear Caroline and Dad chatting away companionably while I bustle around the kitchen, and it's not until I walk over to join them at the table that I notice their conversation has dropped in tone and volume.

"Well, I'm sure she still thinks very highly of you," Dad is saying as I put a pitcher of fruit juice down with three glasses. Caroline's face still has that haunted, shadowy look on it and I feel a peculiar urge to put her at her ease, jumping in to back up my dad's words with a reassurance of my own.

"Pamela Kaufman loves everyone," I say, stoically. "And I'm sure she must like you very much to trust you with bringing our casserole over to us. I'm surprised she didn't come herself, just so she could check that Dad is still behaving himself." I grin at him but am surprised to see confusion on both the faces that are turned toward me.

"We weren't talking about Pamela," Dad says, reaching for Caroline's hand and giving it a paternal squeeze. "We were talking about Anna Chambers."

Caroline sniffs loudly and I see her large doe-eyes blinking back tears as she busies herself with pouring out drinks for us all. I remember the way Anna favored Amy at the diner today and sink down in a chair next to Caroline, letting out a long sigh.

"What has that witch done now?"

"It's not Anna!" Caroline says quickly, sniffing back her tears and speaking in a strange, high-pitched voice. "It's Amy Callaghan. She's decided she wants to be Anna's best friend - Anna's only friend - and is taking on all the bridesmaid responsibilities I was supposed to be doing. She's now maid of honor, which was supposed to be...I mean, with Bella out of town..." She pouts. "It's like Amy sailed into Westhaven and Anna's forgotten anyone else exists."

"She's probably just excited to have her old friend back in town," I say, wondering why for the life of me anyone would be upset about being freed from the burden of the Anna Chambers bridezilla experience. "I'm sure once the day of the wedding actually rolls around things will be different."

Caroline sighs, tracing a line of condensation down the edge of her glass with one perfectly manicured thumbnail.

"Anna told me not to come to the rehearsal dinner in a few days. She said with Amy here now the numbers will be off-balance, so she's given her my seat and I'm not needed." She lifts her head, plastering on an insincere smile. "Which is fine. I mean, it's just the rehearsal dinner. It's not like I'm out of the whole wedding." She jumps to her feet and hurries over to the stove. "That stew does smell good. I'll dish up, shall I?"

Dad takes a long, slow sip of his drink, then meets my gaze.

"It's almost enough to make you feel sorry for her, ain't it?"

"For who?" I scoff. "Amy? Anna? They deserve each other." I pull a face. "But Caroline..." *She was never quite as mean as her friends. And without them to lead the way, I'm not entirely sure what would become of her.*

"I wouldn't worry," Dad says, with a grim smile. "She was part of that high school clique, wasn't she? Those girls can all hold their own, individually as well as in a group. Caroline Mackie will soon get her own back on anyone she thinks has slighted her, you'll see."

My eyebrows raise in disbelief but Dad seems convinced and I can't help but wonder just how he might be proved right.

Chapter Three

The early morning opening at the diner reminds me why I'm actually kind of glad this is just a short-term gig.

"Ah, Ronnie. Still not a morning person?"

I don't bother to rearrange my features into anything other than a scowl as I turn to greet one of my favorite people in Westhaven - and one who really should know me better by now.

"I assume that means I shouldn't ask you for a favor?" TJ grins at me, then holds out a takeaway cup of steaming coffee. "Even if it comes with a gift?"

"I think that's called a bribe," I say, taking the cup and sniffing it suspiciously. A sweet, syrupy scent hits my nostrils and makes my stomach rumble. Getting here early enough to open certainly doesn't leave me enough time to think about breakfast first. I hungrily take a sip of coffee and feel my mood immediately brighten. "But I accept. Even though I am aware that the fact you have this means you've been supporting one of the Slice's many rivals." I arch an eyebrow at him. "Which of those evil corporate coffee houses did you sell your soul to for this?"

"The staff room at the hospital." Now it's TJ's turn to yawn and I wrap my hand a little tighter around my coffee cup in case he dares to ask for it back. "Some generous spirit bought us a coffee machine for Christmas." He frowns. "Or maybe it's just on loan...either way, it got me through a very long night on call."

"You're a pharmacist," I remind him, taking another slurp of coffee before turning back to unlock the door to the diner and ushering him into the building before me. "I thought that meant you avoided all the worst parts of being a doctor."

"Mostly, yes." He grins at me. "But I still have to pull the occasional overnighter if we need cover. And it's Christmas, so we are extra short-staffed this time of year."

"Oh well," I commiserate, hitting the lights and turning up the thermostat until I hear the boiler rattle into life. "There's a lot of that going round."

"Looks like it." TJ follows me into the building and I dance ahead of him before we can get caught underneath Matt's mistletoe. Even with nobody here to witness it, I feel like that would raise the stakes of our friendship a little more than I can cope with this early in the morning.

TJ makes his way towards the counter, pulls out a stool, and collapses onto it, pillowing his head on his hands. "I'll take whatever pastry you can heat up and a hot cup of coffee when you can manage it." He's yawning again and I pause to pat him on the head, which makes him sit up and pull a face at me. "Hey!"

I grin at him as he fixes his hair, making it just the right kind of tousled, and think how grateful I am that TJ is still in Westhaven. He was my best friend all through high school, and even if nothing more than friendship ever happens between us - I'm still not sure if I want it to - it would be a lot harder to readjust to life in my hometown without him here to help me. I take another sip of my drink, then remember the string that was attached to it.

"So come on then, what's this favor you're bribing me into doing for you?" I swallow sadly, wondering what dread fate I've consigned myself to.

"It's about the wedding." He grimaces. "You know. Matt and Anna's?"

"Is there any other wedding happening this Christmas in Westhaven?" I gesture to the empty diner. "Why do you think I'm the one opening up at stupid o'clock this morning while Matt gets to do wedding prep and enjoy his last few days of freedom?" I'm joking, but TJ isn't smiling, and the last few mouthfuls of sweet coffee turn bitter in my mouth. I think I know what's coming, but it's still horrible to watch TJ reluctantly form the words.

"I have to work an extra shift. I won't be able to go with you." He winces and if I didn't know that he was looking forward to this wedding about as much as I am - which is *not at all* - then I might even believe he regrets it.

"But...but you were supposed to be my plus-one!"

"I know." TJ at least has the grace to look disappointed. "And I so wanted to be there..."

That's too much. He's fighting hard not to smile and I decide he needs some payback for dropping me in it. If there's one thing worse than attending your best friend's wedding to your worst enemy, it's being forced to do it solo. There's nothing else for it. I toss my empty coffee cup at him. He laughs and dodges my feeble aim and the cup - which wasn't quite as empty as I'd thought it was - lands with a splat on the floor. I groan and reach for the mop.

"Please tell me you are at least doing something worthwhile with this badly timed extra shift. If you're bailing on me to do a stock take of the high street pharmacy closet or something…"

"I'll be at the hospital again." TJ sighs. "Like I said, it's Christmas and we're really short-staffed. I'm sorry, Ronnie. Genuinely."

"It's fine." *Even though it isn't.* I toss my dented cardboard cup into the trash, then mop the last of the mess up, buying me a precious few minutes to rearrange my expression before I have to look at TJ again. It's not his fault that he's ditching me, not really. And it's only a wedding. I know it's not a big deal. But I have been dreading Matt and Anna's coming nuptials and knowing TJ was going to be by my side the whole time was the one thing getting me through. I draw in a breath and manage to look somewhat normal when I lift my head. "I guess I'll just have to find some other knight in shining armor to protect me."

The door to the diner swings open as I say this and a familiar warm voice reaches my ears before I can turn and greet the new arrival.

"Did you call?"

I roll my eyes as the newly appointed sheriff of Westhaven - Seth Foster - strolls into the diner and smiles at me. It's not a bad smile. Not a bad face - ok, if I'm forced to admit it, he's one of the most handsome guys I've ever seen in real life. Unfortunately, he seems to be acutely aware of this, and no matter how good he looks or how charming he can be there's something about him that continues to get under my skin.

"Ms. Swan."

"Sheriff." I make a point of sliding my mop in a wide path back behind the counter and hear the grunt that passes for a friendly greeting between him and TJ, which is enough to pull me back out to do my job. The last time TJ and Sheriff Foster were together, one had arrested the other on suspicion of murder. At least that isn't likely to happen again today. "What can I do for you this morning?"

"Well, I just came in here for a coffee, Veronica, but it sounds as if you're in some kind of trouble." He raises his eyebrows at me. "Tell me, is there a dragon you need slaying? Some ruffian wants dispatching?" He jerks his head almost imperceptibly in TJ's direction but I continue to stare at him wondering if it's about time I added *crazy* to my assessment of the handsome sheriff.

"What?"

"You're on the lookout for a knight in shining armor." He draws himself up to his full height, adjusting the sparkling silver sheriff's badge he has pinned to his chest, and salutes me. "Ma'am."

I'm actually sort of struck dumb for a moment until I hear TJ's muffled *puh-leeze* which is all it takes to remind me I'm not exactly the biggest fan of Seth Foster or his would-be charm. I cross my arms.

"Not today, thank you. Did you say you wanted a coffee?"

"I'll take three, please. Got to arm the troops." He pointedly selects the next but one stool to TJ and leans against it, not actually sitting down, and rests one elbow on the counter. I now have an audience of two silently judging me while I set the coffee machine whirring and it's only when I catch sight of the clock that I'm able to forget about them. When Matt asked me to open up this morning, he definitely expected me to get things up and running sooner than this. I dash into the kitchen and fire up the oven, throwing in a tray full of flash-frozen pastries to warm through as I check the refrigerator for all the food prep I did last night in advance of my early morning. Silently sending past-me a thank you for being so organized, I'm soon into the flow, and by the time I swing back into the diner to pour coffee I'm greeted by an almost civil conversation taking place between TJ and Sheriff Foster. *It's a Christmas Miracle!* I think, until my attention is caught by the arrival of another customer, then another, and another. The morning rush is in full swing when TJ takes his leave and I wave him off with a promise to call him later. I know he's heading home to sleep and from the exhaustion I can see etched into his face, I don't blame him. Sheriff Foster has gone too, back to the station to greet his deputies with fresh coffee and win yet more admiration from the townsfolk. I sigh. Everyone in Westhaven seems to love the new arrival, and I have to admit he did help me out of a sticky spot when I first came back to town and found myself in the middle of a murder - but his attempts at investigation almost ended up in my friend TJ wearing the punishment for a crime he didn't commit. It's not so easy to forgive or forget that. Plus there's just something I don't trust about him. Maybe if he wasn't quite so handsome.

"Good morning, Ronnie!"

I turn at another familiar voice - Westhaven is full of them - and smile as my friend and once-upon-a-time teacher, Melissa Barnes, staggers through the door, her arms laden with packages.

"I'm on my way to the post office!" she exclaims, her eyes bright and cheeks pink from the outdoor chill. "Got to get these orders out before the last posting date or there are going to be a lot of disappointed customers come Christmas Day!"

Ms. Barnes may have been my favorite teacher but she didn't stay at the high school for long. Now it seems she makes her living running her own small business selling all sorts of weird and wonderful lotions, potions, and supplements that I'm more than a little wary of trying. Cleaning supplies, I'm happy with. But anything with the word *tincture* or *extract* makes me a little nervous. I'm sure they're harmless enough, but without FDA approval and with TJ's numerous lectures ringing in my ears I'm happier to be an encouraging bystander than an active participant in Melissa's latest money maker.

"I suppose you can't share what's in them," I say, nodding at her parcels. "Or you'll spoil my Christmas surprise." I've seen a similarly shaped, suspicious-looking package sitting under the Christmas tree at home with my name on and I'm sure it came from Melissa via my father. I just hope it isn't anything with *essence of toadstool* in the ingredients list.

"Oh no, dear! Yours is nothing more than a handmade gemstone necklace, but I wrapped it up inside a handmade decorative paper box that is just darling, and - oh dear!" Her face falls. "Now I've gone and spoiled the surprise myself. Bother! Oh well, forget I said anything, Veronica, and think of - of - socks. That's what it is! A pair of dull as ditchwater knitted socks."

"Don't fault getting socks for Christmas, now, Ms. Barnes!"

Dad has made his way through the crowded diner to greet me, and he winks as he passes Melissa. "What is it I always say,

Ronnie? Christmas won't be Christmas without a new pair of socks waiting under the tree!"

We both laugh. It's become a standard joke over the years that I buy my father as many pairs of zany, fluffy, and downright ridiculous socks as I can. I've been slacking a little this year and make a mental note to get online and start ordering as soon as my break time rolls around.

"I'm going to go sit over there, Veronica." Dad waves a box of newly purchased Christmas cards. "You come and join me when you can."

"You'd better get those written quickly," Melissa says, with a sharp look in my direction. "I told you the post office is shutting up shop pretty soon if you want them to arrive before Christmas."

"As long as they arrive sometime before *next* Christmas we'll call it good enough, won't we, Ronnie?" Dad winks at me and continues on his way, spotting a lone empty table and claiming it as if he owned the place. Which, once upon a time, he did. "I'll have my usual when you get a minute," he calls, and I know that means firing up the skillet for a bacon sandwich to go with his decaf - doctor's orders - coffee. I wonder if I can sneak something green into his sandwich without him noticing, but then decide that it is Christmas, after all, and what's the festive period without a treat or two?

Another customer approaches the register before I have time to get started on my dad's sandwich and I greet the stranger with a bright smile.

"Good morning and welcome to the Slice of Life diner! What can I get for you today?"

"Ah...information." The stranger must see my expression fall because he hurriedly places another order. "And a coffee. Small. Black." He eyes the crowded diner. "To take away."

"Coming right up."

There's something odd about the newcomer. He's dressed all in black as if he's trying a bit too hard not to stand out. In Westhaven, where people go out of their way to brighten the winter chill with festive colors, his plan backfires.

"Are you new to town?" I ask, politely. "Visiting family?"

"No." The man shakes his head and then nods. "Actually, yes. Sort of." He draws in a breath. "I'm looking for Amelia Callaghan."

"Amelia...do you mean Amy?" I pop the lid onto his takeaway coffee and hand it over, holding my hand out for the cash he has carefully counted out for me. He keeps a tight hold of it though, his eyes widening at my words.

"Amy." He nods, eagerly. "Yes. Do you know her? Are you friends?"

"Ah...not exactly." There's a queue of impatient customers forming behind him, but I haven't the heart to shoo him away. Not until he's paid for his coffee, at least. "I can probably get a message to her, though."

His eager smile falls flat and I can see him wrestling internally before giving me a disappointed nod of agreement.

"Well, I suppose that would be something. Yes. Alright." He takes his coffee from me. "Tell her Liam said hello. No, wait." He frowns, taking a thoughtful sip of the coffee he still hasn't paid for. "Tell her I need to speak to her. It's important. It's a matter of life and death. Or maybe not that. Not quite life and death. But...it's important, anyway. I need to speak to her. Oh!" He seems to remember he's holding my money and hands it out to me with a smile that undoes all the anxiety of a moment earlier. "Here you go! Keep the change." He salutes me with his cup. "Merry Christmas!"

"Merry Christmas to you, too." I glance down at the handful of small coins he's given me and realize that not only will there be no change for me to keep, but he's ten cents short on what he ought to have paid. I open my mouth to call after him but he's disappeared, melting through the crowd of eager customers and out into the chilly day.

Well, that was odd. I can't think of a pair less likely to be friends than Amy - *Amelia* - Callaghan and...this guy. I shrug, filing the information away in the back of my mind, and promise that if I don't see Amy myself to tell her I can get Matt to pass on the message when he arrives. *If he ever arrives...* I force myself not to look at the clock and instead focus on work and soon I don't have time to think about anything at all but food and drink and the smiling faces of a crowd of eager customers.

I might be a little late, Matt had said. *But I'll definitely be there before eleven.* The clock is showing a quarter past when the door finally swings open and I'm so ready for a break I'm already pulling at my apron strings and rattling off my handover to Matt before I realize the person who's marched boldly up to the counter isn't my six-foot-tall male friend, but a short brunette with an attitude. She's a picture of elegance and would be strikingly pretty if it wasn't for the scowl she's wearing. *Amy.* Her phone is pressed to her ear and she's speaking through gritted teeth so I only hear a word or two.

"No, *you* listen. I tried to be patient. I tried to be understanding but it just isn't working, so now I'm removing myself from the situation. We're done. You need to let it go. I'm moving on, and you can just - oh, threatening me now? And a very Merry Christmas to you too!" She jabs fiercely at the handset to end the call then clutches her phone to her chest, bending her head and blinking away a few tears before she can bear to look up at me. In an instant her expression changes, ice melting into sunshine and she beams at me.

"Good morning! Virginia, isn't it? I'm Amy, Anna's best friend. She and Matt have been a little held up. She asked me to run along here and tell you." She shrugs her shoulders in an impish little bounce. "Such are the trials of wedding prep! But now that she has me here as her maid of honor I know things are going to go off without a hitch." She giggles. "Well, you know what I mean. Ouch!"

The crowd of eager diner customers surges forward and one poor unsuspecting coffee drinker stands on Amy's foot, earning a scowl that would be a lot more fitting on a goblin than an elf.

"Watch where you're standing, you idiot! These shoes are expensive!" She turns to me and smiles again, before glancing at the window. Something she sees makes a shadow momentarily darken her sunny smile and I brace for another outburst, but this time brightness wins out. "Oh, it looks like Anna needs me. I guess a best friend's duties are never done. Ta ta!" She waves her elegantly-gloved hand at me and dances out of the diner again. This time the crowd part ways to let her pass after witnessing the suppressed rage lurking under her dainty exterior.

"Nice to see you too, Amy," I call softly at her retreating back, realizing, too late, that I never got the chance to pass on Liam's message. *I might have done it if she'd let me get a word in edgewise.* My lips purse at the memory of her *I'm Amy, Anna's best friend!* introduction and wonder if she remembers we already met yesterday.

I wearily re-tie my apron strings and get back to taking orders. If Matt has been delayed then my break is going to have to wait, and these hungry and thirsty customers aren't all going to serve themselves.

Amy's visitor and her angry phone call nettle me though. I can't help but reflect on how effectively she's elbowed Caroline out of Anna's inner circle and I imagine just how successful she would have been at doing that if Bella was still in town. The idea of those two squaring off against each other is enough to make me shudder and not just because of the gust of icy wind that blows through the diner every time someone opens the door. I don't think even Westhaven could survive that much mean-girl energy.

It's probably a good thing that Bella won that cruise and left town for Christmas, then. Anna's wedding - and Westhaven itself - has been spared a real festive disaster!

Chapter Four

B usiness at the diner isn't bad, especially not at this time of year, but we are definitely once more in the festive version of a lull when Matt finally strolls in, as the light outside is starting to dim and the dozens of strings of fairy lights that adorn every inch of Westhaven at Christmas are adding a warm, cozy glow to the view.

"I'm late. I know. I'm sorry."

If it was anyone else throwing those words at me instead of offering a genuine explanation I might have been annoyed, but with Matt I have learned over the years to let a lot of things slide. Like leaving me solo running the diner for more hours than I'm happy with. *Like his choice of fiancée.* I'm still not used to the idea of Matt and Anna being a couple and I wonder if actually seeing them take their vows will change that for me. I remember the dismissive look Anna gave me the last time we met. A lot of things might have changed since we were in high school, but certainly not Anna Chambers and her attitude. Which is why I just cannot for the life of me figure out what sweet, stupid Matt sees in her.

"What's the matter?" he asks, coming back out of the kitchen wearing an apron and trying to smooth out the worst of his hat-hair. "Let me guess. You want a real apology." He plants his feet and folds his hands in a prayer-pose before making his best puppy-dog eyes at me. "Please forgive me, dearest Ronnie, for leaving you running the diner without backup for so long today. It was a cruel and unusual sort of punishment, especially this close to Christmas, and - hey! This place is looking pretty good." He turns a slow circle, noticing how neat and tidy I've managed to keep things behind the counter, and how many platters of pastries, cakes, and cookies are now boasting sad-snowman *Sorry, all out!* placards on them. "Did you really sell all this stuff?"

"I certainly did. And I even rang in an extra order of breakfast supplies ready for tomorrow. Tim's going to deliver them in a couple of hours."

"Have I ever told you that you are my favorite temporary casual new employee?"

"I am your only temporary casual new employee," I remind him, tugging at the strings of my apron. "And I am long overdue for a break."

"You know, if you switched from temporary to permanent and casual to full-time, you'd get a lot more out of this job..." Matt's voice is wheedling and I can't quite tell if he's joking or not. He seems to take my hesitation as encouragement. "Come on. You can't tell me you don't love this place. Isn't it just like being home again?"

"It is," I admit. "But that's more on my dad's poor parenting than anything else." I grin as I remember how many long hours I spent hanging out in this very diner while I was growing up. With Matt, who always felt like a big brother to me. A brother who seems bound and determined to walk down the aisle and wed the worst person I know. I grit my teeth. "So what were you doing all day while I was here keeping *home* afloat?"

"Wedding stuff." He pulls a face and reaches for the last of the white-chocolate-snowman-melts I was saving for my break. If he notices my frown, it doesn't stop him from shoving my cookie into his mouth and swallowing it practically without stopping to chew. "You have no idea, Ronnie, how much goes into organizing a wedding. Especially one at Christmas."

"Especially one that involves Anna Chambers," I mutter under my breath.

"What's that?"

Apparently I wasn't quite as subtle as I meant to be and I hurry to smile before poking him in the ribs.

"You ate my cookie. Just for that, I'm taking all the tips we got today." I up-end the Slice of Life mug we leave out for the more generous-minded of our customers and palm a handful of loose change. "I earned them, anyway."

"You certainly did. Hey, Ronnie?"

I stop counting my tips and look at Matt, who grins at me. "Thanks."

"You're welcome. I'm expecting to see your gratitude reflected in my pay check."

"Of course." Matt is affronted at the suggestion he would be anything other than generous. "And think about what I said about staying on here. More permanently, I mean. I know I said I don't need a partner but that doesn't mean I'm not looking for a great new employee. We work well together, don't we? And if you stuck around here, it'd be kind of like old times."

The thought is a tempting one, but I only get a moment to enjoy it before the reality of our present times comes crashing through the diner door, talking loudly with her friend.

"Do you really think we can do it ourselves, Amy? I mean, it's a lovely idea and I saw the clip you showed me but really, I do want everything to be perfect."

"Exactly, darling. What's more perfect than doing it all yourself? And you're so creative, Anna. This is your chance to put your own stamp on the wedding. Right, Matthew?"

Amy turns to wink at Matt as she says this, and he makes an eager nod, stammering something in the affirmative as if he has a single clue what Amy and Anna are talking about.

"See? Matt agrees. It's a great idea."

"What is?" I match Amy's tone almost exactly and pitch my expression at just the right degree of interest but seem to successfully fool nobody because if Matt's glance my way is confused, Anna's is flat-out irritated.

"Wedding favors. I've decided to make my own."

"Aren't you leaving it a little late?" I check the date on my phone, even though I know full well what day it is, and just how many are left before I lose Matt forever. Once he's *Mr. Anna* that will be an end to all our old times, and right then and there I know that no matter how tempting a picture he paints of us working together at the Slice, it won't be like that. It already isn't now, whenever Anna is in the picture.

"We've got plenty of time," Anna says, stubbornly. "We're just going to call in at Maeve's Store to pick up a few ingredients. And Pamela Kaufman is dropping in all the equipment we might need." Her eyes dance with something that might be mischief but reads to me more like defiance. "We're going to bake gingerbread. An individually baked and iced cookie for every single person attending the wedding. Isn't that a lovely idea?"

I sense Matt tense next to me and choke back my reply. I did promise I'd try to get on board with his soon-to-be bride but then I remember how easily Anna cast Caroline aside in favor of this new-old best friend of hers.

"We?"

"The bridesmaids." Amy smiles at me, but the expression doesn't reach her eyes, which remain cold. "And a few other specially-chosen friends and family members."

"That sounds nice," Matt says, sensing the tension between me and the other two, and stepping in to disperse it. "Hey, do you girls want to use the diner? We could close up early, and..." I hear more than a few pointed coughs from our regular customers and decide that if Matt wants to turf people out early into the cold, dark night that's on him. I'm glad I pocketed my tips when I had the chance because that kind of decision doesn't win anybody's generosity.

"Now, Matthew, why would we need to use your diner when we have a perfectly nice house of our own - well, Anna's own? We have a kitchen and everything!" Amy lets out a musical little laugh and I side-eye Matt, wondering if he's surprised by how comfortable Amy seems to be making what's Anna's hers as well. Again, I think of Caroline and wonder if there's room in the Amy-Anna house of best-friendship for her at all.

"Well, don't let us delay you," I say, my voice ringing with false cheer. "You've got a lot of gingerbread to bake, after all." My breath catches and I remember one detail I have to share that I've been particularly dreading. "I'm afraid it'll just be one for me. I just found out today that TJ won't be coming after all."

"Won't he?"

I hear the question from Anna and Matt in stereo, but what might be a vindictive curiosity in Anna's voice sounds like concern in Matt's. When I look at him I see worry that quickly shifts to practiced indifference before anyone else can spot it. I smile and hope I sound more light-hearted about TJ's abandonment than I feel.

"He got called into work," I explain. "So I guess I'll be flying solo. But at least that's one less gingerbread cookie for you and your army of bridesmaids to make!"

Anna smiles, but the expression isn't exactly genuine. Amy is clearly bored by any conversation that doesn't concern her, and she whips out her phone, tapping out a message before sliding it away again and slipping her free arm through Anna's. That seems to be all the cue Anna needs to get back into action, and after blowing a noisy kiss at Matt the two hurry out of the diner and into the dark, chilly night. Matt watches them go, but he doesn't seem to miss my glance because his features relax into a wry smile.

"Well? Are you going to take that well-earned break or not?"

I don't need telling twice, and I've yanked the apron back over my head before Matt has a chance to change his mind.

• • • •

IT'S PROPERLY DARK by the time I make my way home from the diner, but with the lights from several neighborhood homes and trees to light my way as I walk through the town, I barely feel the chill in the air. Instead, the magic of Christmas is all around and I wonder how I can have gone so many years away from this tiny little town, especially at this time of year.

"Yes, Ma, I understand. No, I'm not doing this deliberately, but -"

I hear the sheriff's voice before I see him, and I am too close to his shadowy figure to get out of the way before he steps backward into the street - and directly into *me*.

"Ouch!"

"Oof! Hey!" He swings around, spots me, and realizes his mistake almost immediately. "Gotta go, Ma." He ends his call, takes a courteous step back, and smiles. "Sorry 'bout that, Ms. Swan. Hope I didn't cause any damage."

"None that can't be remedied." I briskly re-tie my scarf and look around, trying to work out where he's come from. The sheriff's station is all the way across town, and we've reached the edge of the high street where all of Westhaven's most notable eateries - like the diner - are. This street is purely residential, or so I thought. A jumble of laughter bursts through an open window and I hear the faint strains of a classic Christmas song and that's when I realize Sheriff Foster isn't dressed to fight crime. He's dressed for a party.

"Don't let me keep you from your celebrations," I say, as the laughter from inside the house dies down enough that I can make out a voice asking *where Seth has got to*. "I think your friends are looking for you."

"Aw, let 'em look." He rolls his eyes. "I'm only here to make up the numbers anyway." He drops his voice, sneaking me a mischievous grin. "It's a work thing, and I'm still new enough that I'm trying to make sure they all like me."

Well, it seems to be working, I think, but don't say. Westhaven isn't generally all that welcoming to newcomers but somehow they seem to have taken this one to their hearts.

Nowhere more so than the sheriff's department itself, and I know he's already a favorite amongst deputies, departments, and admin staff alike.

"You aren't traveling home for Christmas?" I haven't yet managed to ascertain exactly where *home* is, and I have to admit I'm curious, despite myself.

"Ah, no. Duty calls. Your friend TJ isn't the only one pulling extra shifts over the holiday period." He realizes he's still got a tight hold on his phone and sheepishly shoves it into a pocket. "Much to my mother's disappointment."

I can't picture Sheriff Foster's mother, but the idea of her intrigues me and I hope she doesn't feel too miserable without him home to celebrate the season.

"You needn't worry about Ma Foster," he says, reading my thoughts with that weird intuition he seems to possess that I suppose makes him a good detective, objectively speaking. "I'm only one of half-a-dozen. There will be plenty of other people for her to fuss over without me there adding to the number."

"I'm sure she'd like to see you, all the same." I smile, politely. "Maybe for the new year."

"Maybe."

We stand in silence for a moment until I start to feel the chill of the night air and wonder why Seth - lacking my hat, scarf, coat, and gloves - doesn't seem to notice it.

"Well -" I begin, as Seth speaks at the same time.

"So how about you? All set for Christmas?"

I'm surprised he wants to keep talking to me but for some reason, I don't brush off his question. If he's happy to stand here in the cold and dark and make small talk I suppose I can spare a few minutes. After our interactions over the last few months, it'll probably do me some good to get the sheriff back on side. I'm still not sure he doesn't hold me responsible for the messy murder business that happened the very same week I rolled back into town.

"It will be a very quiet one at the Swan household this year," I say, pursing my lips. "If I can persuade my dad to actually stay at home and rest like he's supposed to."

Seth grins. He's met my father and they seem to get on like a house on fire, which is all the more peculiar when I think about how hot and cold he blows with me.

"I suppose yours will be too, if you're stuck here in Westhaven working." I have a strange urge to ask him to join us, feeling sorry to think of him spending Christmas alone, but he speaks again before I can.

"And don't let's forget the wedding of the year." He sounds about as excited for Matt and Anna's nuptials as I am, and when I roll my eyes he laughs. "I'm surprised you're not at this gingerbread-making party. Sheena was raving about it all afternoon, and promised that if it wasn't Extremely Important Wedding Business she'd never think of passing up our work party to go and help out." He winks. "Between you and me I think she's just excited to be asked. Never would have thought her and Anna Chambers the type to be close."

Sheena? I realize he means his deputy and think back to the over-eager rule-follower I remember from high school.

"They aren't!" I bite my lip. "They weren't. When we were teenagers…" I trail off. Sheriff Foster has heard my tales of the Anna, Bella, and Caroline and their reign of high school terror before now, and he doesn't approve. The concept of people changing - or in this case, not changing at all - is one we're going to have to agree to disagree about.

"I guess that explains why you aren't there. Considering how close you and Ms. Chambers...aren't."

"I didn't even score an invitation." I grin at him. "As you can tell, I'm truly devastated by the oversight. I suppose I'll have to wait until the wedding itself to see this amazing gingerbread in all its glory. Are you -"

But before I can finish my question a scream pierces the chill night air. I turn in the direction of the noise, certain I imagined it, but then it comes a second time, then a third, followed by other shouts and exclamations.

Sheriff Foster is moving before I am, and I follow him, stupidly, moving towards the commotion that spills out onto the street from one of the prettily decorated houses not too far away from us. It takes me a minute to place the people - all of them women, and women I recognize - until my mind works to recognize Caroline Mackie. Tears streak down her face, which is pale and blotchy with crying, and her voice comes out strangely high-pitched and breathless.

"Oh! Sherif Foster! Thank goodness it's you! You have to come quickly. There's been - there's been a murder!"

Chapter Five

There's such a lot of chaos and so many people crowded into Anna's elegant living room that I'm sort of grateful I can blend into the crowd. With EMTs on the scene, Sheriff Foster has gone straight to work, enlisting Sheena - Deputy Dell - to help him. She seems more than eager to leap into action, complete with her fluffy apron and hen-party hair extensions. Their attention is fully focused on the investigation and I think he's forgotten I'm even here.

"Veronica? It's just so awful!"

I feel hands clamp around my shoulders and barely resist being pulled into a full-body embrace by Pamela Kaufman, who clings to me like a life-raft.

"Mff-nff-gfff."

She lets go of me a little, and I'm finally able to turn my head enough that my words are no longer muffled into her shoulder.

"Are you ok?"

"I wasn't here when they made the discovery!" She sniffs. "I'd just run out to my car to get a bag of groceries to go with the box of equipment I'd dropped off earlier. I sent Caroline in ahead of me, and she went into the kitchen with Anna, and they...they..." I see her lower lip quiver and hastily pull her back into an embrace, feeling her shoulders heave with sobbing.

With Pamela hanging off me, I try to peer around the room to see if I can spot Caroline and Anna. I see lots of shocked faces of friends and neighbors I recognize, but it isn't until Deputy Dell's voice rises above the whispers that I catch sight of the pale, tear-streaked face I'm looking for. Anna seems stunned, her features pinched and painful, and I notice Caroline standing staunchly beside her, with a thin arm wrapped tightly around her waist.

"We'll need to take everybody's statements as quickly as we can. If you've already spoken to Sheriff Foster or myself, please make your way over to this side of the room." Deputy Dell gestures like a traffic attendant, and I watch Anna and Caroline drift over to that side of the room, their eyes wide as they stare unseeing at the rest of us. "Everyone else," Sheena continues, with all the subtlety of a foghorn. "Please form an orderly line on this side of the room."

"Deputy." Sheriff Foster sticks his head in from the kitchen, frowning when he sees her attempts to bring order to the chaos of Anna's living room. "What are you doing?"

"Organising the witnesses," Sheena chirps. "Like you told me to."

"I told you to take everybody's details," he says, sweeping the room with a glance that comes to rest on me. "Everybody who was here at the time of the incident, I mean." He arches one eyebrow and I make a show of patting Pamela Kaufman gently on the shoulder as if to justify my reason for being there. If Seth's sore at me for finding myself in the middle of yet another murder investigation, well, he'll just have to deal with it. I'm not one to abandon a distraught woman, especially not when she's clinging so tightly to my neck it's close to cutting off my air supply.

"Oh, sorry, Veronica dear," Pamela murmurs, as I try to extricate myself from her grip. She sucks in a breath and straightens, then offers me a watery smile. "I'm quite alright now." She pauses, appearing to recognize me for the first time. "I didn't know you were joining us this evening. When did you arrive?"

"I was just passing," I say, pointing to the door. "I was outside when Caroline - when the sheriff..."

"Ms. Swan?"

As if Sheriff Foster has heard my whispered conversation, he barks my name and beckons me forward. I hesitate but there's something in his look that suggests I'd better do as I'm told and I give Pamela one last encouraging pat on the shoulder before picking my way carefully past the crowd of other women to join the sheriff in the kitchen. He bends down over something, reaching out with the edge of a handkerchief to lift something small and sparkling from where it lies on the floor and I squint at it, trying to work out what he's found. A bit of Christmas tinsel? Glitter? No, it's a piece of gold chain.

And that's when I spot the body.

It's hard to think of the tangle of hair and limbs and blood I see crumpled on the floor of Anna's picture-perfect kitchen as *Amy*. The room spins and I feel myself sway before strong arms reach out to steady.

"Easy," I hear the sheriff's comforting voice low in my ear and force my head to turn away from the image that I know is going to sear itself into my brain. I may not have liked Amy much - at all - but that didn't mean I wanted to see her dead. "You know you don't need to be here for this," he says, steering us to the one corner of the room where our view is blocked by the refrigerator. "You probably *shouldn't* be here for this." He frowns, and I wonder what's worrying him until he reaches for his phone. "Let me call someone to get you home."

"I'm fine," I protest, feeling the truth of the words becoming truer as my heart rate returns to normal. "Really." I smile, or try to, and will myself to be convincing. "I'll walk. It isn't far."

The sheriff looks as if he's about to say something more, but Sheena's shrill voice pipes up first, echoing around the house.

"Ok, you can all form an orderly line, and I'll start taking everybody's name and contact details..."

There's something officious and almost eager in her tone and I think for a moment she's in her element, which is surprising when everyone else that's here right now is a shell-shocked mess. Even Sheriff Foster, who must have seen his fair share of crime scenes, seems unsettled by his colleague's present work ethic. I spot the hint of a frown on his face, but he notices me notice him, and the look is gone, swiftly replaced with a mask of professionalism.

"In that case, Ms. Swan, I'll say goodnight. As you can see, I still have a crime scene to secure."

· · · ·

"RONNIE? IS THAT YOU?"

By the time I get home, it's late and I can tell Dad's worried by the quiver in his voice. I hurry into the living room where he's wearily climbing out of his chair and lay a calming hand on his shoulder to tell him to stay put.

"It's me. I'm sorry I didn't call to let you know I was going to be delayed."

His gaze travels to the clock on the wall and he frowns.

"Something happened on my way home from the diner." I pull off my scarf, kick off my boots, and start shrugging out of my jacket, grateful for the warmth of the electric fire as I inch towards it and hope it'll start to ease the chill that settled in my bones that's got more to do with murder than the winter temperatures. "Do you remember that friend of Anna's who came to town? Amy?"

"The one who's taking over the wedding, you mean?" Dad's frown darkens. "Put poor Caroline's nose right out of joint, hasn't she? What's she done now?"

I'm surprised to see Dad coming to Caroline's defense, but then recall that I've been softening towards her a bit lately as well. Then I'm reminded just who's niece Caroline Mackie happens to be and I wonder if there might not be a bit more than mere paternal chivalry behind his interest in her wellbeing.

"Have you...have you heard from Pamela Kaufman this evening?" I try to keep my voice light, remembering that my father is still recovering from a heart attack, and certainly wouldn't benefit from any sudden shocks.

"Why?" Dad's eyes narrow in suspicion and I realize my attempt at deflection isn't working at all well. "Has something happened to Pamela?"

"No! Nothing at all." My smile freezes. I remember first seeing her pale, anxious face in the crowd of women who all flew at Sheriff Foster when he reached Anna Chambers' house - with me following curiously behind him - and think *nothing at all* might be downplaying things a little too far. I sigh, realizing there's nothing for it but to tell the truth, as quickly and simply as I can. I draw in a breath, but before I can say a word Dad's phone starts to ring. An absurdly cheerful Christmas jingle pours into the room and he guiltily lifts the handset, tilting it so he can see Pamela Kaufman's smiling face in the caller-id display. His expression changes almost imperceptibly and I see him struggle to resist the urge to immediately answer. He looks up at me and I could swear I see a blush on his thin cheeks. It's getting harder and harder to deny that the friendship between my father and Pamela Kaufman is veering ever closer to romance, and I'm wondering if this latest crisis might be just the thing to clinch it. I sigh, fighting a smile, and point to the phone. "Aren't you going to answer that? I'm sure Pamela Kaufman can tell you what's happened just as easily as I could." I pull a face. "With plenty of detail to go with it."

Dad lets out a bark of laughter but obediently lifts the phone to his ear.

"I hope you aren't suggesting Pamela's a gossip, my dear. Because she has only the nicest things to say about you..." He shifts his tone into what I like to refer to as his Clark Gable voice, and answers. "Good evening!"

I drift into the kitchen, happy to let Pamela do the telling of this particular tale. I hear my father's voice morph into something soft and comforting and smile to myself as I start rattling pans, just so he doesn't forget I'm still in the house.

When I first came back to Westhaven and noticed the peculiar degree of care Pamela Kaufman took for my dad as he recovered from his heart attack I was amused, then mildly horrified by the idea of them becoming an item. But whether they are or aren't, there certainly seems to be a friendship between them that they both appear to cherish.

An image of TJ floats through my mind and I reach for my phone, surprised that his wasn't the first voice I wanted to hear after learning what had happened to Amy. *What happened to Amy*? I sink back against the counter, staring dumbly at my screen while my thumb hovers uselessly in space. I'm not sure what to tell him or where to even start. My screen bursts into life before I can press it, and I hurriedly slide to accept the call, pressing the handset to my ear and I'm surprised when it isn't TJ's voice on the other end of the line, but Matt's.

"Ronnie?"

He sounds anxious, and I find my own nerves climbing - the very opposite of the comfort I'd wanted to find from the next person I called.

"What's up?" I try to keep my tone light, even though I don't feel it. "H-how's Anna?"

"How do you think?" I know it's worry, not anger, making Matt's voice clipped and irritable, but it still stings. He seems to notice it at the same time because he mutters an apology that's only half-covered by his sigh. "Sorry. It's just awful, Ronnie. Anna is devastated by the whole thing, and of course now we're trying to find somewhere else for her to stay, what with...what happened at her house."

Right. Anna's home is now a crime scene. I bite my lip, thinking that I wouldn't want to spend the night in a house where a murder happened, either.

"Everywhere is booked out. Between Christmas and the wedding, Westhaven is full of extra bodies - ah, extra people." Matt pauses and I hear voices in the background of the call. When he comes back he sounds relieved that at least one problem has been taken off his plate. "She's going to stay with Caroline. Good. That's something. But listen, I think I'm going to need to be around tomorrow when the police - she's going to need me with her. And I know you spent all day at the diner today, but do you think…?"

"Of course," I say, knowing what Matt is going to ask before he forms the words. "I'll open up and close, the same as I did today. Don't worry about that."

"Thanks." I hear the relief in his voice. "You're a lifesaver."

My stomach lurches as I think again of Amy, dead, and I end the call without saying anything else. *A lifesaver? Not exactly.* I may not have been on the scene when this murder happened but I can't help but feel a little bit responsible for it. I knew there was something off about Amy's arrival in Westhaven, and my intuition was telling me that something bad was going to happen. *I just didn't think it'd happen to Amy…*

Chapter Six

News about Amy's death has settled over Westhaven like a black cloud the next day, and despite the festive decorations that light up the town, the high street is a shadow of its usual self. Even the diner is deserted, and after my mad dash to open up ready for the anticipated crush of morning regulars, I'm left with only myself to cater for. I'm beginning to wonder if something else has happened that I haven't heard about yet when the door opens and I see Caroline, bleary-eyed and tousle-headed but otherwise looking like her usual gorgeous self.

"Good morning, Veronica!" She yawns, then pulls one over-sized mitten off and then another as she stumbles into the diner. "I'll take coffee to go, please. Two - no, three." She smiles at me. "One for me and Anna, of course, and then a third for Matt." She frowns. "I assume you know how he takes it? I forgot to ask."

"I'll figure it out." I nod towards the stools that line the counter in front of me. "Come sit down a minute and I'll get you all set up." I work swiftly and in silence, waiting until I have all three coffees made before I risk a glance in Caroline's direction. She's perched on the stool I indicated, tapping away at her phone, and there's the slightest hint of a smile on her face. If I didn't know better, I'd think she looked almost...happy.

"Three coffees," I say, waving her away before she can even offer to pay. "On the house."

"Oh!" her large blue eyes widen. "That's so generous of you!"

"Well, it's generous of Matt." I wink. "And I don't think he'd thank me for charging him for a cup of coffee from his very own diner, do you?"

Caroline looks momentarily confused, then shakes her head, offering me a real smile as she slides her phone back into her purse.

"So what are you guys up to today? Matt asked me to cover his whole shift." I try to look sympathetic, rather than curious. "I suppose Anna is taking everything pretty hard."

"Hm? Oh, yes. She's devastated." Caroline takes a noisy sip of her coffee and then smiles at me. "So I'm taking charge of things. There's still so much to do for the wedding, and now - well, let's just say I'm going to have my hands full getting everything finished on time." She turns towards the door and I hurry forward to open it for her, surprised and a little unnerved by how unconcerned she is about what happened last night.

"Is the wedding still going ahead then?" I blurt out. "I mean -"

"Of course it's going ahead!" Caroline pulls a face at me. "Why on earth wouldn't it?"

"Well, after what happened to - to Amy," I say carefully, wondering if Caroline has slipped so deeply into shock she doesn't remember what she witnessed the previous evening.

"Oh, that." Caroline shakes her head. "Yes, it's very sad. But it's certainly not going to stop Anna and Matt from getting married. I won't let anything derail their happy day." She steps out into the drizzly morning and waves at me. "Trust me, Veronica. Nothing is going to stop Anna from getting exactly what she deserves!" She pauses and for a minute my blood feels cold in my veins before she lets out a musical little laugh. "Her happily-ever-after, of course!"

"Of course." I smile, but the expression doesn't feel convincing and I watch Caroline's back retreating down the deserted high street for a long time, feeling unnerved and unsure of what to do about it.

I'm still puzzling over the peculiar interaction when TJ arrives, sliding past me into the diner and looking around in surprise before his gaze comes to rest on me.

"Matt really must be unhappy with you! What have you done to get stuck on the early shift twice in a row?" He's pulling off his hat and heading for the very stool Caroline just vacated when he realizes I haven't immediately followed him. "What's up?" He nods at the empty chairs surrounding him. "Where is everybody?"

"You haven't heard?"

"Heard what?" TJ leans over the glass cabinet and helps himself to a gingerbread cookie. He eats half of it in one large bite then grins at me. "What? Why are you staring at me like that? Look, I know cookies for breakfast aren't exactly top-tier adulting, but I'll have you know I worked another night shift - because apparently my boss and yours are in cahoots to make us both exhausted and miserable right in time for Christmas, and - hey!"

I fly across the cafe and snatch the free half of the gingerbread cookie out of his hand before sliding it onto a plate and hastily brewing up another pot of coffee I can split between the two of us.

"There was a -" I hesitate, trying to recall the non-murder word Sheriff Foster had used when he called the station to make his report the previous evening, but I come up blank. "Something happened last night. Somebody died."

"Who?" TJ's eyebrows lift and I know he can tell from my anxious energy that this is serious. "Where?"

"At Anna Chambers' house."

This makes TJ's eyebrows lift even higher and he swallows the rest of his bite of cookie in stunned silence.

"It wasn't...I mean, she's alright, isn't she? Anna?" TJ looks a little pale and I see all at once that he wonders if I'm covering for Matt because he's dealing with the fall-out of losing his fiancée only days before their wedding. I shake my head, eager to reassure him.

"Anna's fine." I remember Caroline's unnaturally happy attitude and hesitate. "Physically, she's fine. It was her friend. The new one. Old one. Whichever. Amy Callaghan." I draw a shaky breath and repeat the detail that won't stop niggling at me whenever I think about what happened the previous night. "Somebody killed her. I mean, I think they did."

"So it's a murder?" TJ takes one of the two cups of coffee I place down on the counter and takes a ponderous sip. "Well, at least nobody can accuse me of any involvement this time. I have a rock-solid alibi." He winces, hearing the relief in his words about the same time I do. "Sorry."

I shake my head and reach for TJ's hand, giving it a friendly squeeze. I remember how horrible it was when he was swept up in the investigation of the last murder to happen in Westhaven - right when I first came back to town. *And now it's happening again.* I shiver, despite the warmth of the diner, and wonder if I'm the common denominator between the two.

"So who has Sheriff Foster got his eagle eye on this time around?" TJ lets go of my hand and reaches for the last of his cookie before cramming it in his mouth. "I'm assuming he's already busy rounding up suspects." He pulls a face. "Is that why the diner is so quiet? It's not like this Amy person went out of her way to make friends since she came into town."

"That's no reason for anyone to kill her," I snap, but again I'm reminded of Caroline's breezy attitude, and how all of a sudden things seem right between her and Anna in a way they hadn't been since Amy first strolled onto the scene. *That doesn't mean anything,* I protest. *She's just making the best of a bad situation. And it's good that Anna has someone on her side. She'll need it, with all this happening in her own house. And so close to the wedding. And -*

"Uh oh." TJ takes a sip of his coffee and eyes me warily. "I know that look. You're going to involve yourself in this murder the same way you did the last one, aren't you?"

"Certainly not!" I glare at him, then reach for a second gingerbread cookie. I snap it in half and drop it onto his plate, before choosing a piece to munch on. "I wasn't there when it happened." My mind is still whirring with possibilities. I may not have been there when it happened, but I was there straight after. And I may have more insight than Sheriff Foster into just what was going on behind the scenes. In the short time she was in Westhaven, I certainly witnessed several different sides to friendly, dismissive, beautiful, bad-tempered Amy Callaghan. My eyes narrow. *And the weird friend who came to town looking for her.*

"Well, good. It's not like any of us even knew Amy what's-her-name. Before she swanned into town and shoved Caroline out of the spotlight as Anna's resident best friend I'd never even heard of her. Had you?"

I shoot him a withering look, and he grins.

"What about Matt? What was his opinion of the new arrival?"

"He liked her," I say, although I can't be too sure that's true. Matt has been surprisingly tight-lipped about Anna's supposed oldest friend. "And I know she didn't know a lot of people in Westhaven but someone in town knew her." I close my eyes, trying to conjure up the stranger who had come into the diner the previous day asking after her. *What was his name?* "Liam!"

TJ looks at me, then lays a hand on his chest, speaking slowly and clearly as if I'm an idiot.

"My name's *TJ*."

"No. I know. There was a guy in the diner yesterday asking about Amy - Amelia. He called her Amelia, and said he'd come here looking for her." I frown. "I don't think he was local." I remember the strange way he was dressed, and the desperation in his face when he struggled to decide what message to leave. "He was a bit funny."

"Funny ha-ha? Or funny weird?"

"Weird." I shudder, remembering how disconcerted I felt by his sudden appearance and disappearance. "Definitely weird. And I never got a chance to pass his message on, anyway."

"Maybe he found Amy all by himself." TJ's voice is low, scarcely more than a whisper, and I feel the chill in the air settle deep into my bones. "Maybe this Liam guy is our killer."

I glance at the clock, then survey the empty diner. I'm supposed to stay here and run the place all day, and I promised Matt I'd be fine with that, but I wonder if he'll object to me taking on an apprentice, just to buy me an hour or two of free time. Because if Sheriff Foster hasn't heard of this stranger who came to town looking for a girl who just turned up dead, it's about time he does.

* * * *

"I THOUGHT YOU DIDN'T want me rushing around on my feet all day?" Dad asks as I tie an apron around his more-than-ample middle. "Isn't running the Slice of Life diner in the middle of the Christmas rush the opposite of *rest and recuperation?*"

"Would you rather stay sitting alone at home with nothing to do and nobody to talk to?" I ask, throwing the words of his own complaint back at him. "Breathe in!" He obediently sucks in his gut and I manage to get the strings of the apron tied into a bow. "Now, you don't have to stand up. I'd rather you didn't." I run around the front of the counter and grab a stool, dragging it to sit behind the cash register. "There. Sit. You can take orders if anyone comes in, and you should be able to make the odd coffee and sandwich. You remember how to do it, right?"

"Ha!" Dad rolls his eyes. "Listen, young lady. I was running this place single-handedly before you could even walk -"

"Great!" I drop a kiss on his cheek. "Then you'll manage just fine while I take my break." I dash towards the door. "I'll just be a quarter of an hour. Remember! No rushing around. Slow and steady."

"I'm sure I'll manage," Dad says, drily, as he surveys the near-empty diner. It still isn't a patch on the usual Christmas hustle and bustle but for once that's a good thing, and I know I'm leaving the place in very capable hands. I just wish I didn't have to.

You don't have to, a voice nags me. A voice that sounds uncannily like that of the new sheriff. *This isn't your murder to solve, you know. You don't need to go hunting out clues or tracking down suspects, or...*

"Veronica!"

I halt at the sound of my name and turn to see Melissa Barnes hurrying towards me.

"Did you hear what happened?"

"I know," I say, sadly. "Isn't it awful?"

"Dreadful." Melissa shakes her head. "As if Pamela Kaufman is capable of such a thing!"

"Pamela Kaufman?" I hesitate, trying to make sense of the unexpected change in direction. I'd assumed Melissa was talking about Amy's death. What on earth did Pamela Kaufman have to do with anything?

"Melissa," I say, patiently taking her by the arm and steering her back towards the diner where I know Dad is working, oblivious to the news that Pamela might be in some kind of trouble. "What's Pamela Kaufman done?"

"They think she's responsible for killing that poor young friend of Anna's. Bludgeoning her to death. It's completely ridiculous, of course!"

"Completely," I agree, shuddering at the thought. "Why on earth do they think Pamela is responsible?"

"Because it was her rolling pin," Melissa says. "And you know what Deputy Dell is like when she latches onto an idea. She's tenacious."

"That's a polite way of saying stubborn as a mule." I push the door open and scoot Melissa over the threshold. "Come into the warm and we'll work out what we're going to do."

"What you're going to do about what?" Dad isn't sitting on the stool I pulled out for him. He seems to have decided that this is the perfect moment for a little stealthy furniture rearranging and I dart over to him and wrench a pile of three chairs out of his hands.

"About reminding myself that you can't be left alone for a minute!" I glare at him, then point back to the stool by the cash register. "What were my instructions? Sit still, rest, and take orders from eager customers when they arrive."

Dad opens his mouth to protest, then spots Melissa and relinquishes his hold on the chairs.

"Melissa! You look like just the sort of eager customer my daughter was telling me about. Come in and sit down, won't you? I'll get you something to drink. Tea's your poison, isn't it?"

"Tea *without* poison, if you don't mind, Edgar." She sighs and wearily begins unwrapping the first of many layers she's wearing to ward off the cold. "There's been enough death already without adding me to the mix, although I dare say Pamela would welcome some company at the sheriff's station..."

I shake my head sternly but Melissa isn't quick enough to see it, and Dad has already latched onto the one name that I knew would make his ears prick up.

"What's that?"

"Pamela Kaufman is giving her statement at the sheriff's station," Melissa says. It must be ever so stressful, but I'm sure she has friends with her. And Caroline, of course."

Melissa's features twist but before she can say any more Dad's in full white-knight mode. He tugs at the untidy bow I tied in his apron strings and haphazardly shrugs out of the thing, stalking towards the door.

"I'd better go and see what's the matter," he says, looking worried. "You don't mind, do you, kiddo? I'll be back once I know everything is sorted out."

"I don't think it'll be that easy -" I protest, but in the end it's Melissa who lays a restraining arm on Dad's back and urges him to wait.

"Come on, now, Edgar. What are you going to do? Burst into the sheriff's station and demand Deputy Dell lets Pamela go? When she's still being questioned?"

Dad frowns.

"You know that will just get everyone's back up," I jump in, moving around to Dad's other side. Between us, we escort him back to an empty table and sit down on three empty chairs.

"Exactly. And you can trust Sheriff Foster. He certainly won't allow anything bad to happen," Melissa continues, speaking low and slow, as if Dad's a scared cat she's trying to rehabilitate. "I'm sure this is just part of their investigation. They have to look at everything, after all. And you and I both know that Pamela Kaufman is a lot of things but she isn't a murderer. And if she was, she wouldn't use a rolling pin. Or any kind of kitchen equipment. It's...it's..."

"Unsanitary?"

Dad glares at me, but Melissa nods, sagely.

"No, you're right. Pamela was fastidious about her kitchen - and her equipment. She never would have even let it out of her sight."

I hesitate, recalling what Pamela sobbed into my shoulder the night before. She had let it out of her sight. Her box of kitchen equipment had been dropped in to Anna's house long before she'd even arrived that evening. Pamela might have owned the rolling pin that was used to kill poor Amy, but she certainly hadn't been the person delivering the fatal blow. And I can make sure Sheriff Foster - and the over-eager Deputy Dell - knows that. *And I can remind them that there are other suspects to look at than friendly neighborhood ladies. Like the mysterious Liam who was so desperate to track Amy down...*

"I'll go," I say, jumping to my feet. "You stay here and make Melissa her tea. Have a cup yourself. I'll just run along to the station and see if I can't find out what's happening."

Chapter Seven

Knowing I don't want to leave Dad too long, even with Melissa there to keep an eye on him, I head straight for the sheriff's station. When I burst through the door there's no sign of Pamela. I assume she's holed up in one of the interrogation rooms to the side of the waiting area, and having spent an hour in one of them myself before now I feel a flash of sympathy for the older lady. I don't see any sign of Westhaven's team of deputies but I do see a few familiar faces. Sitting in a line along one side of the room are Caroline, Matt, and Anna, all looking pale and bleary-eyed. Anna and Matt stare miserably at the ground, and Caroline is flipping through a stack of old travel brochures someone has left in the waiting area. None of them look my way, so I walk straight toward the reception desk, finally catching sight of the very person I want to see as I do so.

Sheriff Foster seems unsurprised to see me bypassing the queue of people waiting to speak to him, and I brace for yet another lecture about involving myself in crimes that are none of my business.

"Don't you people have homes to go to?" He looks at Matt, then me. "Or businesses to run?" Then Anna. "Weddings to plan?"

Anna makes a shuddering sigh and Matt automatically reaches an arm around her but says nothing.

"Sheriff!" I blurt out, catching him as he's about to disappear back into the bowels of the station.

"Veronica." He turns and blocks the door with his whole body, stopping me from going any further into the building. It's a trick he's used before, and I'm beginning to think he keeps it ready to use against me, specifically. "What can I do for you this morning?" He glances at his watch. "Pardon me. This afternoon." He offers a crooked smile and my stomach growls, alerting me to the fact that it's after lunchtime and I need to eat something. *Well, food can wait. I need to make sure Pamela's ok, for Dad's sake if nothing else.*

"I want to speak to you about Pamela Kaufman."

"Really? Are you a family member?"

I open my mouth but before I can respond Caroline rushes over to join me, with an impassioned plea.

"No, but I am! I'm her niece. And - and I don't think she should even be here. She has nothing to do with what happened to Amy."

"You seem very confident of that, Ms. Mackie." Sheriff Sam's gaze slides over to Caroline without blinking. "You were there last evening as well, weren't you? In fact, I believe it was you who was with Ms. Chambers when the body was discovered."

"That's right." Caroline nods, and I'm surprised to see her grow in confidence, rather than wilting the way I expect her to. "And I know for a fact that my aunt didn't arrive until later on." She glances at me and I see a glimmer of triumph in her even features. "So she couldn't possibly have had anything to do with the murder."

"And the fact that she owns the equipment that was used...?"

"She brought that over to make gingerbread!" Anna's voice is feeble but determined and all three of us turn to look at her as she lifts a tear-stained face to look at us. "She loaned it to me so that we could make favors for the wedding. She brought it over early and left the full box in the kitchen. Whoever attacked Amy must have found it and just used whatever came to hand." She sniffs, noisily, and I see Matt's arm tighten almost imperceptibly around her thin shoulders. He's stoic, supportive, and his expression remains taut and unreadable. I don't know what sort of a reaction I'm expecting but he offers none until Anna turns to him for confirmation. "You remember? You said we could use the kitchen at the Slice but I told you I wouldn't need to because we were going to use the house. We bought ingredients from Maeve's but Pamela insisted on lending us her Women's League equipment. She came to help out, that's why she was even there to begin with. Everyone else at the house last night was my particular friend, and only there because I wanted them there. Except..." Her gaze rests on me and I feel as if the air gets sucked from the room. "Except for Veronica. You turned up right after we found - after we found Amy. Almost as if you knew."

I feel the color drain from my face, even though I know Anna's accusation is baseless and unfair, and I know Sheriff Foster won't believe a word of it. *I hope.* But Matt is the person I'm looking at, and when he doesn't leap to my defense I feel my heart sink. *So much for friendship.*

• • • •

"ALRIGHT, VERONICA. What else did you want to talk to me about?" Sheriff Foster is sitting across a narrow table from me. It's not the first time he's escorted me into one of the station's empty interrogation rooms for a conversation, and I have a sinking feeling it won't be the last. "Or did you just want to escape that awkward little exchange out in the waiting area?"

"Both." I sniff, but to my surprise, I see a flicker of something that might be sympathy in the sheriff's dark eyes. The glimmer of light is gone in a moment though, and I'm left wondering if I imagined it. Then he opens his mouth and confirms it.

"You still haven't won Anna Chambers over then." He winces. "She doesn't like you much, does she?"

"The feeling is mutual." I lay my palms down carefully on the table in front of me, then worry that being quite this candid is a recipe for getting myself on a list of suspects I don't want to be on. "Which does not mean I broke into her house and attacked her friend."

"I'm glad to hear it." Sheriff Foster looks amused. "Is that it? You came all this way to tell me something I already knew?"

"No." I shake my head. "I came to tell you that if you think Pamela Kaufman had something to do with this then you're completely mistaken. She wouldn't hurt a fly."

"I have several bitter members of the Women's League that would say otherwise."

"But why would she attack Amy Callaghan? She didn't even know her before a couple of days ago. None of us did."

"Anna Chambers did. And just because Amy was new to Westhaven doesn't mean she didn't cause some disruption simply by being here." He makes a show of shuffling some papers, then leans back in his chair. "I believe she made Ms. Mackie more than a little miserable, for example."

"So?"

"And Caroline Mackie is Pamela Kaufman's niece."

"If you're suggesting that because Amy took Caroline's place on the top table at a wedding, her aunt decided to commit a murder..."

"It's a theory."

"It's a stupid theory." I didn't mean to say that last part out loud, or certainly not loud enough to reach the sheriff's ears, but I catch another flicker of amusement in his eyes that suggests he not only heard every word, but he agrees with them. He turns to a fresh sheet of paper and looks expectantly up at me.

"So what's your alternative? Come on, Veronica. You do have a theory, right?"

He's teasing me, but then I remember I did manage to solve a murder last time, and maybe my ideas are worth considering, whether he thinks so or not.

"I think you should look at who might want Amy Callaghan dead."

"I thought nobody in Westhaven even knew who she was before a couple of days ago." He's using my own logic against me, but little does he know, I have a suspect lurking just off-stage. Fighting the urge to smile, I march the specter of Liam out on display.

"Somebody came to Westhaven looking for her."

"Is that so?" This has surprised him, and even though his mask of calm is back in place with barely a moment's disruption, I notice the slip and feel a flicker of satisfaction. *Score one point for the amateur sleuth.*

"A guy called Liam...something...came into the diner asking about Amelia - Amy - Callaghan. He seemed pretty keen to track her down. Desperate to talk to her, even." I make a show of folding my hands in my lap. "If *I* were investigating this crime, I'd start by looking at him."

"Liam Something." The sheriff's lips quirk. "A mysterious stranger who seems uniquely qualified to be a suspect in a case. Perfect timing, Ms. Swan. Just the thing to get your friend Pamela off our radar. Anything else you'd like to share that might help track this phantom friend of our victim's down? I don't suppose he left you his number for Amy to call, did he?"

"He didn't." I slump back in my seat.

"Can you at least give me a description?" He is poised to note down whatever I say, but unfortunately, there isn't much.

"Uh...medium height, maybe? Medium build. Brown hair. Kind of...unremarkable." One detail reasserts itself. "Oh, he was wearing all black. He looked kind of ridiculous. Like he wanted to blend into the background but he was trying a bit too hard."

There's a brief moment of silence.

"Or maybe he just likes the color," Seth mutters, brushing a bit of lint off the sleeve of his own all-black outfit. *Oops.*

"Maybe." I don't say anything else. What else is there? The only thing remarkable about that Liam guy was that he was so...unremarkable. The exact opposite of the sort of man I would have pictured having any kind of connection with Amy Callaghan.

The sheriff lifts his head, eyeing me expectantly in case I think of anything else to share. I shrug.

"Sorry. We had a five-second conversation and the diner was busy." I sigh. "But maybe you could ask Anna if she knows anything about him. Maybe Amy mentioned a friend who was meeting her here in town."

"Nope." Sheriff Foster makes a note or two on the page in front of him, then smiles in that vaguely disarming way he has. "We asked her and she said there was nobody. Amy came all the way to Westhaven to see her and celebrate her wedding. No other reason. No mystery guy, that she was aware of. But thanks all the same."

There's a knock at the door to the small interrogation room we're using and he looks up as Deputy Dell pokes her head into the room, glancing nervously from her boss to me and back again.

"Uh, Sheriff, you might need to come back out here..."

An unexpected wail from the seating area propels Seth to his feet and I follow before he can tell me not to, so we both arrive in time to see Anna throw herself into Matt's arms, leaving Caroline and Pamela awkwardly clinging to a huge bouquet of expensive-looking flowers.

"What's going on?" Sheriff Foster takes in the tableau in confusion before turning to Sheena for an answer. "Deputy?"

"Well, I had a colleague check out Anna's house, you know, before she goes home. Wanted to make sure it was safe for her to return, and...well, they found these flowers waiting by the front door. I told them to bring them to the station. I thought Anna might like to see them. I know if someone sent me flowers as lovely as these..." She stammers an answer, shooting her boss a look that borders on defiant. "Anyway, I thought it'd be a nice thing to do. Only, turns out...they're not addressed to Anna at all."

"Who are they meant for?" The sheriff asks, even though I think he already knows whose name is on the small card that Sheena now grips tightly in one hand. There's only one that could dissolve Anna back into a sobbing mess like this.

"They were sent to Amelia Callaghan." Sheena quietly passes the card to her boss, who takes it and glances over it before looking sharply in my direction. He clears his throat before reading the contents of the small card aloud.

"To my sweet Amelia, please forgive me. We can make this work if you'll just let me explain. Love, Liam."

Chapter Eight

"**I**t's all so very awful!"

Pamela Kaufman manages a weak smile that reassures my very anxious father that she isn't going completely to pieces. They're sitting together in a quiet corner of the busy diner, and I keep a careful eye on them from my spot behind the counter. There's no persuading my dad to rest and relax, but at least this means he's sitting down, and I can tell Pamela is grateful for his support.

"If I didn't know better," the sly voice of Melissa Barnes says at my elbow. "I'd say that no matter how awful it all is, Pamela rather likes being the center of attention."

"Even if it places her at the center of a murder investigation?"

"Not her." Melissa winks at me. "Her rolling pin."

"Drink your tea." I know she's joking but I would find the whole story a lot more amusing if I wasn't so worried about my dad's blood pressure. It's one thing to discuss a murder in the theoretical; it's something else entirely when someone you care about is caught up in it.

I plate up two hot brie and cranberry sandwiches and take them over to where Dad and Pamela are sitting and going over the horrors she endured at the hands of Deputy Dell at the sheriff's station.

"I know they're considering everyone who might have a motive or an opportunity. That's what detectives do when there's a crime to solve, don't they? Even poor Veronica came in for a second look, although Sheriff Foster soon dismissed that, didn't he, dear?"

I nod.

"He's such a nice man, Seth. He certainly seems to have his head screwed on alright. Not like that deputy of his." Pamela sniffs noisily into a tissue. "She was so nice to me the other day, helping me drop off my box of cookware to Anna's house ready for baking. But today!"

"I'm sure she's just trying to do her job," I say as I put the two plates down. I'm no great admirer of Sheena Dell, but she's nothing if not efficient. *Too efficient.* I remember how quickly she leaped into action once she figured out those flowers weren't for Anna, but for their murder victim, and I wonder just how long it will take her and Sheriff Foster to track down the mysterious figure of Liam Wright. At least they have a surname for him now, and probably a credit card receipt from Betsy's floristry store. This will all be resolved in no time.

"Well, at least now they have a sensible lead to follow," Dad says, echoing my thoughts. He takes a bite of his sandwich and urges Pamela to do the same. "This boyfriend, or whoever he is. He sounds like a piece of work, alright."

I shiver, remembering Liam's presence here in this very diner, and wonder if anything I might have said or done then could have kept him from finding out where Amy was. *I might have helped keep her alive.*

"Are you alright, Ronnie?" Dad catches sight of the change in my expression and pulls out a third chair. "Sit down a minute. When did *you* last eat?"

"I'm fine," I say, but my stomach growls and in the end I accept his offer, perching for a minute in the free chair and taking the second half of his sandwich. I chew and swallow methodically, even though I barely taste it, but it does help me to feel better.

"I just won't feel safe until they catch that - that monster!" Pamela trills, sniffing back another round of sobs.

"Aunt Pamela?"

The door to the diner swings open and Caroline bursts in. She flies to Pamela's side and throws her arms around her.

"I was so worried about you!"

"And I was worried about you! That wretched deputy kept asking me if I thought it possible that you held a grudge against that poor dead girl!"

"Really?" Caroline stiffens and steps back, her grip on her aunt tightening until it looks almost painful. "What did you tell her?"

"Well, I told her it was ridiculous. Oh, dear, you are squeezing me! There, that's better. You sit down here next to me and Mr. Swan. We were just talking about this horrid boyfriend that followed poor Amy all the way here..." Pamela shakes her head. "It's quite unnerving to think of him stalking her around the place and then hurting her like that. Dreadful. And Westhaven is such a lovely little town!"

I bite my lip to keep from reminding her this isn't the first murder our *lovely little town* has seen lately. *And it probably won't be the last.* I'm not sure where that thought comes from and try to shake it off by focusing on the case at hand.

"Where's Anna?" I try to weigh my words with concern, rather than curiosity. "And Matt?"

"They went home." Caroline bristles a little. "Deputy Dell insisted they didn't need me there. She was going to walk through the house with them and make sure everything was alright."

There's an awkward moment of silence before my dad breaks it, exchanging a brief look with Pamela.

"Well, that's nice of her."

"It's a little presumptuous." Caroline folds her arms, glancing irritably at her watch. "We have all sorts of wedding tasks that need sorting out - last minute things, you know - but she actually tried to suggest that *she* could help Anna with anything that needed doing this afternoon." She sniffs. "*I'm* the maid of honor."

"I'm sure she just wanted to help Anna feel more relaxed," I suggest, getting to my feet and collecting the empty crockery from the table. "You know, if she's afraid this Liam guy might come back."

"Who?" Caroline looks up, confusion making her forehead crease. "Oh, yeah. Him. Well, I think Sheriff Foster said he was going to look into that. He said you gave him some really useful information."

Dad and Pamela both look at me, surprised, and I feel my cheeks flood with heat. *Useful information?*

"He was probably being sarcastic," I say, spotting the shadow of another figure approaching the front door of the diner. Our usual footfall is way down, but it isn't nothing, and I am supposed to be running this place while Matt's away. I want to make sure I do have some regular profits to report. I stand up, ready to make a dash for the cash register to take the next order and mentally rehearsing what I can upsell. Super-sized coffee? Gingerbread cookies? A late lunch?

"Caroline, you sit down for a minute and have something to eat and drink," Pamela says, tugging her niece down to sit on the chair I just left. "You've got a busy afternoon ahead of you. Are they still planning to do the rehearsal dinner tonight?"

"Oh, yes." Caroline hops up again, oblivious to her aunt's fussing. She strides towards me, pulling her phone out in front of her to consult it. "That's what I meant to tell you. Matt decided it would be better for everyone if we did the rehearsal here, after the church bit I mean. He told me to tell you to close up early and arrange all the tables like this." She angles her phone towards me and I squint at a badly taken photograph of a scribbled floor plan. I only get to see it for a second before a message illuminates Caroline's phone and she snatches it away again, but not before I happen to see the first couple of sentences.

"If you don't get me that money I'm going to make sure everyone knows about what you did to Anna. Don't test me - I mean it!"

• • • •

WITH THE REHEARSAL dinner relocating to the Slice I'm even more eager to shut up shop early and head home. I can't stop thinking about Caroline's menacing phone message, even though she seemed to laugh it off quite easily. The few words I read keep bouncing around my head. *I'm going to make sure everyone knows about what you did to Anna.* What did Caroline do? The curiosity eats at me, and it leaves me distracted all afternoon. I'm relieved when quitting time rolls around and I can start packing things up for the day. The sooner I'm out of there, the better. Even the Slice's most committed regulars can't argue too much when I explain that the owner needs the space for important wedding business.

"It's nice that they're still going ahead with the wedding after that awful business with that poor young girl getting hurt, isn't it?"

Charlie Rollins, one of the Slice's regular customers, is determined to milk every last second he can out of the diner this evening. He has been following me around for the last ten minutes while I've moved around the place cleaning up and wiping down surfaces.

"Here, Veronica. Allow me." In a surprising display of chivalry, he takes hold of a table I've been struggling to shift and easily slides it alongside its neighbor until I have a long, straight row down the center of the diner.

"Thanks." I straighten and wipe my hands on my apron, surveying the room. "Does this look like a top table to you?" He stares at me, non-plussed. "Anna and Matt want to have their rehearsal dinner here. I want to make sure everything is ready. Or as ready as it can be." I glance towards the kitchen, wondering if the selection of cold buffet food I pulled together will meet with the bride's exacting standards. Matt didn't exactly give me much of a warning about the change of plans, and I certainly don't plan to stay here and single-handedly cater hot food for a cast of however many.

"You are asking the wrong person." Charlie grins and slicks his thinning grey hair over to one side. "I got married all of one time a hundred years ago. Didn't take. Never was tempted to try it again." He salutes me and heads out into the night, leaving me alone to make a few finishing touches to the diner before I shut off most of the lights and lock the door behind me. I want to be long gone before Anna arrives, and it's not as if I have a role to play in the rehearsal. *Unless you count making myself scarce!*

I hurry home, eager to see Dad again and settle down for a quiet evening of job hunting and wrapping the few meager Christmas presents I have ready to stack under our tree. I'm more than ready to put this murder business out of my mind for a few hours and have even managed to convince myself that I've blown Caroline's mysterious threatening message out of all proportion. If she isn't worried about it why should I be? Better I focus on the bits of the holiday season I enjoy, and those I still need to organize. It will be a quiet Christmas at the Swan household this year, but after the drama of the last forty-eight hours, I'm actually kind of looking forward to it.

I hear the crunch of footsteps on the asphalt behind me and glance over my shoulder, seeing only the shadow of a figure. I continue to walk and hear the footsteps pick up their pace, then slow. I frown, then vary my own steps, only to hear them mirrored behind me. When I glance a second time over my shoulder the shadowy figure is a lot closer than I remember, and my heart begins to beat hard in my chest.

You're just imagining things, I try to tell myself. *You can't be the only Westhavener eager to get home on a cold night like this one!* I hear a faint door slam somewhere, and then the footsteps start up again. It reminds me of another person intent on acting like my shadow earlier today and I let out a shaky breath of relief before turning around.

"Charlie, you have to stop following people around. It's one thing when you're helping me shut down the diner, but out here, I -"

My voice cuts off automatically when I realize the person who is following me isn't Charlie at all. But whoever they are, they're definitely following me.

The figure steps into the light and my blood runs cold. This man's facial features might be unremarkable, but I'd recognize him anywhere. *Liam Wright.*

"Wh-what are you doing here?"

"You're Amelia's friend, aren't you? You work at the cafe?"

"The diner." My voice sounds strange and strangled and I swallow past a lump in my throat. "Veronica Swan."

"Where's Amy? Did she get my flowers?"

Liam looks paler than when I last saw him. He's still clad head to toe in black, and now I notice dark shadows under his eyes that add to his menacing appearance. He looks exhausted. *And desperate.*

"What do you mean? You must know where Amy is. You must know what happened..." I manage, glancing around to my right and left, wishing for Charlie - or anybody! - to step out of the shadows right about now and help me.

"I don't know anything, she refuses to speak to me!" Liam's shout sounds even louder than it truly is in the quiet of the night and I take a step backwards. "Wait, sorry. I'm not - I didn't mean to -"

"Everything alright over there?"

My heart leaps and I think, of all the voices belonging to all the people in Westhaven, right now this is the only one I want to hear.

"Over here!" I wave, taking a step towards it and praying that my next words are enough to scare Liam off me for good. "Sheriff Foster! Maybe you can help us out?"

Liam looks around and when he spots the figure of the sheriff moving cautiously towards us, his eyes narrow. He doesn't run, which surprises me. But then I suppose there's no accounting for crazy. *And he'd have to be crazy to stick around in Westhaven after what he did to Amy.*

"Ms. Swan." Sheriff Foster smiles at me. "I might have known you'd be causing trouble on a quiet night like tonight. What's up?"

I take a hasty step towards the sheriff, and if he notices he doesn't have time to react before Liam speaks again, his voice ringing with urgency and panic.

"Sheriff. Thank goodness. You can help me, I'm sure. I'm t-trying to find someone. My girlfriend. She's disappeared, she won't return my calls, and I just want to make sure she's ok." He draws in a shaky breath. "Amelia Callaghan. Maybe you've seen her?"

I sense rather than see the sheriff's body tense and he positions himself in front of me, closer to Liam.

"You'd be the mysterious Liam Wright, I suppose." He glances at me and I nod, not taking my eyes off the stranger. "Well, I guess that makes tonight my lucky night. We've been looking for you."

"Looking for me?" Liam sounds genuinely confused. "But how did you know...I mean, why were you looking for me?"

"Perhaps you'd like to accompany me to the station," Sheriff Foster says, making the kind of request that sounds more like an order. "I have a few questions I'd like you to answer." He pauses. "About the murder of Ms. Amelia Callaghan."

Chapter Nine

"That's it. No more walking to and from work alone for you."

My dad leaps into protective Papa-Bear mode before I even get through telling him what happened on my way home from the diner this evening. We're sitting around the table eating but it looks like Edgar Swan is more interested in laying down the law than eating a meal right now.

"TJ, tell her."

"Tell me what?"

Dad holds his hand up as if to silence me, and applies himself to TJ, who is currently laser-focused on eating his meal. He came to join us for dinner and I had hoped he'd be on my side, but it looks like he's staying as neutral as he can right now. He shovels in forkful after forkful of pasta and swallows almost without chewing and I know my cooking isn't that good. This is avoidance, and it's working.

"Tell me what?" I repeat, and eventually Dad lets out a sigh like he's carrying the whole world on his shoulders and turns to speak to me slowly and clearly as if I'm still in kindergarten.

"It's not safe for you to wander around these streets after dark. From now on, you wait at the diner after your shift until TJ or I can come pick you up." He pauses. "Or you get a ride home with your friends."

"Dad!" I whine, in a tone of voice that completely undercuts my next argument. "I'm not a kid!"

"Yes, you are. You're my daughter and I'm not about to let you get hurt."

"Nothing happened!" I protest. "A guy tried to talk to me and I got spooked, that's all."

"A guy that's currently being held at the sheriff's station on suspicion of murder," TJ points out, slurping a mouthful of spaghetti off his fork.

"Do I need to remind you that *you* were held at the sheriff's station on suspicion of murder not so long ago?"

TJ colors and focuses back on his food, and I turn Dad's raised hand trick against him as I see him gathering more arguments in favor of me being escorted around town like a toddler.

"It looks like this wasn't some random attack. Poor Amy was targeted by someone that knew her, someone that - hopefully - Sheriff Foster now has safely behind bars." I swallow, remembering the relief I felt when he appeared at just the right moment to come to my rescue.

"It's a good job he came along when he did," Dad mutters, his words sinking into something I can't make out.

"Yeah, how did he know where to find you?"

"He didn't." I sigh, tugging awkwardly at a loose lock of hair. "He was on his way to the church for Matt and Anna's rehearsal - running late." I wince. "He'll be even later now."

"He's in the wedding?"

I shake my head.

"Deputy Dell left her purse at the station. He figured she'd need it."

"*She's* in the wedding?"

I nod, equally as surprised by this development as I know Dad and TJ will be.

"She's been promoted to bridesmaid."

"Has she?" Dad frowns. "I didn't know she and Anna were all that close."

"They're not." I take a disinterested bite of my meal. "Or they weren't. But Anna's down to one bridesmaid - Caroline - and I guess beggars can't be choosers."

"She could have chosen you!"

TJ and I glance at each other and manage to keep our composure for all of a minute before bursting into laughter.

"Oh, I know you aren't the best of friends -"

"Trust me, Dad. When it comes to being a bridesmaid for Anna Chambers, Sheena Dell is welcome to the role. It's bad enough I even have to go to the wedding. Alone." I throw TJ a mock glare. "I certainly don't need to take part in it." The very thought makes me shiver. "If I was Anna I might start to think the wedding was cursed. First Bella leaves town, then Amy appears and is dispatched just as quickly. Sheena had better watch out!"

"And Caroline," TJ says, finishing his meal and pushing his plate aside. "I would have thought the coveted role of maid of honor puts her in the firing line more than the newest addition to the team."

TJ's joking, of course, but his words do have a sobering effect on Dad and me. I swallow another mouthful of my spaghetti but my appetite is pretty much gone. After another few minutes, I give up altogether and start clearing away two empty plates and my one that's still half-full. I hear the banter start up again between Dad and TJ as they discuss sports results and plans for Christmas. TJ is driving out to his sister's house late Christmas Eve, ready to surprise his little nieces and nephews on Christmas morning. I feel a flicker of disappointment that with him working the night of the wedding this might be my last chance to see him before Christmas and then realize with a lurch that I haven't even bought him a gift.

"Excuse me a minute!" I announce, dumping the dishes in the sink before dashing upstairs. There must be something in all the boxes of old junk my dad has been digging through that I can repurpose into the kind of nostalgic, thoughtful gift that disguises the fact I haven't thought about it at all. I toss aside school memorabilia, awards, and assignments until my hand closes around the very thing I was looking for. My prom photo. A photo of *TJ and me* at the prom. I smile as I look at it, staring past the awkward pose and our trendy-at-the-time formal wear, and think how grateful I am for this friendship, and the way coming back to Westhaven has breathed new life into it. I do a quick job of wrapping it in paper, then snatch up one of the leftover Christmas cards from the batch Dad and I wrote and sent the other day, and I scribble a few words to TJ. *Tis the season for memories!* I sign it *with love*, then think better of it. TJ and I weren't dating when we went to the prom, and we aren't a couple now, but there's still the possibility of that on the horizon. I wonder, sometimes, if he's as aware of that as I am. Maybe too much time has passed. We know each other too well now. We're well and truly friendzoned. And yet...

Shaking off my rambling thoughts, I dash off an *xo-xo* and seal the card in its envelope, before hurrying back downstairs with the present hidden behind my back.

"Oh, she returns!" Dad is bent over the dishwasher, and as I move towards him he straightens, holding his hands up in surrender. "Alright, alright! I was trying to make myself useful, but I know what you're about to say. I suppose really I should go put my feet up and watch the game. Rest my weary bones. Doctor's orders, right?" His eyes sparkle with mischief and I fight the urge to laugh.

"Go!"

Dad salutes me and grins, before sneaking out of the kitchen and leaving all the clean-up to TJ and me.

"Alright." My friend stands up, stretches, and comes to join me by the dishwasher. "There is a knack to loading these things just right, and luckily for you, it is a knack I have perfected over my long years of living alone..."

"Here!" I can't wait any longer and hold out the present for TJ to take. He's so surprised he doesn't move at first, before finally accepting the gift with a blush that makes him all of a sudden look younger than his years.

"What's this?"

"What does it look like? It's a Christmas present."

"But Christmas isn't for a few more days yet!" TJ looks disappointed. "And I didn't bring anything for you."

"That's ok." I shrug one shoulder. "I figured with you working so much we might not even see each other before the holiday and I didn't want you to miss out."

TJ hesitates.

"My gift can wait until the new year," I tell him. "Just make sure it's a good one, ok?"

He holds out his arms and I snuggle into them, relishing how warm and how comfortable and how *right* they feel wrapped around me.

TJ's phone buzzes against me and as we straighten and part he reaches for it, his features falling as he reads the message.

Something about the action stirs a memory in me and I glance at the clock. It's still early enough that the rehearsal dinner will still be going on at the diner. I remember something Dad said and it triggers worry I've been trying hard to ignore all evening. *I would have thought the coveted role of maid of honor would put her - Caroline - more in the firing line.* But *maid of honor* hadn't been Caroline's role. Not at first. *That had belonged to Bella, until she left town. Then Amy, until...*

"Uh-oh."

I realize TJ has been watching my confusing muddle of thoughts play out on my face, but he hasn't yet figured out the line of investigation I've been mentally pursuing.

"You're already imagining what amazing present I'm going to organize for you when I come back to Westhaven. Well, Ronnie, I can tell you now, it ain't gonna be a pony...ow!"

I punch him on the arm, harder than I mean to.

"Sorry." I absent-mindedly stroke the bruise, still trying to catch hold of the thoughts that bounce around inside my head like a haze. "Hey, you have your car with you, don't you?"

"Always." TJ pulls out his keys and jangles them at me. "Why?"

"Because I need you to give me a ride back to the diner. Now. I forgot something. My phone." I smile a wheedling sort of smile. "I forgot my phone."

"Your phone." TJ frowns at me, and when I look back at him he nods towards the counter where my phone is very obviously sitting. I grab it and shove it in the back pocket of my jeans, then raise my voice so that Dad can hear my comment.

"Yep...my phone. Left it at the diner. You don't mind giving me a ride so I can go pick it up, do you TJ?"

TJ looks at me like he knows I'm up to something but can't tell what, and I shove him in the chest, pointing at the Christmas present he's still holding. *Do this for me and don't ask any questions*, I tell him silently. *That'll be all I want for Christmas this year.* By some miracle he seems to understand me, and nods, slowly, then closes the door of the dishwasher, hitting the button and waiting for it to burble into life.

"Of course I don't mind giving you a ride to the diner," he says, in a voice that rings with stiffness and performance. "Why don't we go right now?"

Chapter Ten

The Slice of Life diner is lit from the inside which gives it a picturesque, holiday-card feel and for a moment I can't help but acknowledge a prickle of loneliness at the sight of the long table filled with smiling, happy faces. I see Matt and Anna, surrounded by friends, then spot Pamela and one or two other neighbors and Westhaven townsfolk I know. Deputy Dell is almost unrecognizable as she bends her head close to Anna's, beaming as she tells what looks like a very long and detailed story. She's playing with a pendant she wears on a ribbon around her neck and Anna smiles politely in response to whatever she's saying about it. They aren't a pair I'd pick for friends but Sheena, at least, seems determined to force a connection. I feel a flicker of indecision and slow my approach to the diner, wondering if I'm making the wrong decision here. Then I catch sight of Caroline. She is the only person at that table not smiling. Her usually bright and cheery face is a mask, blank and devoid of all emotion. She might be sitting in the maid of honor seat next to Anna, but she doesn't look very happy about it.

"Well?" TJ prompts, as he slows to a stop watching me watch the diner. "Are we going in, or what?"

"We're going in." I stride forward, hoping I convey more confidence than I feel. To my relief, TJ falls into step beside me. I put my hand on the door and go to push it open but it doesn't give way, and I slam inelegantly into it. Cursing to myself, I reach for my keys, but in the time it takes me to dig them out of my purse, Matt has noticed us, excused himself from the center of things, and come to unlock the door from his side.

"Hey, Ronnie." He opens the door a crack and blocks my view with his body. He glances over his shoulder and then looks back at me with a smile that is not exactly welcoming. "What's up?"

"I forgot my phone," I say, forcing my features into a stiff smile. "You don't mind if I pop inside and get it, do you?"

Matt hesitates just long enough for me to realize he does mind - or he knows that Anna will - but fortunately this might be Anna's party, but she isn't the only one here.

"Veronica, dear!"

Pamela Kaufman has spotted us and not for the first time in my life she comes to my rescue. "TJ! Oh, how cold you look! Come inside and warm up for a minute. Matthew! Don't keep them out in the cold like that!"

"Yes, and don't linger too long under the mistletoe, fella!"

A couple of Matt's friends hoot with laughter. He rolls his eyes skywards and I feel a little affronted. He was more than happy for me to be in the diner when I was singlehandedly running it the past few days and stringing mistletoe up right by the door was his decision, not mine. I'm reminded of the changes being in a relationship with my arch-enemy has wrought on my old friend, and wonder how much worse things will get once they're actually married. *Not important*, I remind myself. *I'm here for Caroline.* My heart thuds painfully in my chest. Here for Caroline? Or here to stop her from doing something terrible?

"I'll just be a minute," I promise Matt and I sail across the threshold as soon as I feel him ease his grip on the door. "Sorry to interrupt!" I direct these words at Anna with a wave, and it's only out of the corner of my eye that I see the scowl that temporarily replaces her picture-perfect smile. "Hi, everybody! How's the rehearsal?"

"Going off without a hitch," Matt says, as he follows me towards the kitchen, keeping a close eye on both me and TJ. "Or it was until just now."

"I said I'll only be a minute," I mutter, my indignation rising. *But if you'd rather I leave you to spend the evening with a potential killer then maybe I should turn around right now,* I think but don't say. "I'm glad Anna can put that horrible murder business behind her and enjoy the evening." This comes out a little louder than I mean it to, and I hear an audible gasp from more than one dinner guest.

"Maybe your phone is in the kitchen, Ronnie. Let's check, shall we?" TJ takes me by the elbow and practically drags me away from the crowd who are staring daggers at me and it's not until the door swings closed behind us that I hear the low rumble of whispers starting up again. "Ok." TJ folds his arms and glares at me. "So are you going to tell me what we're really doing here? Because I know exactly where you left your phone." He scratches his jaw and I obediently slide my phone out of my back pocket, ready to "find" it the moment I need to.

"I just needed to check something out."

"The rehearsal dinner?" TJ's expression changes to something that might be disappointment. "I know you don't love the idea of Matt and Anna getting married but I thought you were at least resigned to the fact of it happening." His lips twitch like he's about to ask me something else, then thinks better of it. Glancing over his shoulder he surveys the crowd around the table then turns back to me. "I think we've got about another minute in here before people really start to wonder what's going on. So what's the real story, Ronnie? If you want me to back you up, you have to tell me what's going on." He swallows. "Is this about Matt?"

"What?" I'm so surprised I let out a laugh, and then clamp a hand over my mouth. I realize what it is that TJ thinks is upsetting me and the idea is so absurd I almost can't process it. *Does he think I'm in love with Matt Taylor?* When I'm sure I can trust myself to speak I answer him, keeping my voice low in a whisper that won't carry beyond his ears. "You think I'm here because of Matt. What, you think I'm trying some last-ditch effort to stop the wedding?"

"Aren't you?"

I draw in a breath, then decide it's about time I truly trusted TJ with my suspicions. He helped me out last time a murderer was running loose in Westhaven. Why not trust him now?

"I'm here because I don't think that Liam guy had anything to do with Amy's murder. I think the real killer is a lot closer to home. A lot closer to the bride."

"Veronica? Are you ok in there?"

The question doesn't come from Matt but another, decidedly feminine voice, and it's the very person I most dreaded seeing tonight - and most need to. I grab hold of TJ's hand and pull him out of the kitchen and back into the main area of the diner, brandishing my phone like some kind of trophy.

"I found it! I knew I'd left it in here somewhere. Caroline, you're just the person I wanted to see. Can I have a word?"

"About what?" Caroline is all wide-eyed innocence, and I see Anna tense behind her. Part of me is conflicted. I don't want to get Caroline in trouble with her friend, but then I remember just how much trouble she might already be in and I swallow my doubts. *If she is in any way responsible for what happened to Amy she needs to come clean.*

"I think Anna needs to know what's going on. Right, Caroline?"

Caroline sniffs but keeps her gaze averted, and I decide to push just once more. Caroline might have lashed out and ended up killing a person, but I don't think she'd try it a second time. Not in front of a room full of witnesses, anyway.

"Caroline. I think it's about time you tell the truth about what happened."

Caroline sucks in a jagged breath, glances over her shoulder at Matt, then looks back at Anna, her eyes spilling over with tears.

"I'm sorry! I didn't mean to do it! It was an accident!"

Then she turns and runs from the room, leaving us all staring after her in shock.

• • • •

"WHAT SEEMS TO BE THE problem here?"

Even dressed to the nines there's no taking the *deputy* out of Sheena Dell, and she makes straight for where me and Anna are standing. At first, I think she's shifting back into work mode and I open my mouth to explain that what she ought to be doing is chasing after her suspect who basically just admitted to murder. Then she puts a protective arm around Anna's thin shoulders and turns to glare at me.

"Don't you think it's about time you leave as well, Veronica? This is a rehearsal for Anna and Matt's wedding. They don't need anyone here who isn't committed to celebrating their relationship."

My mouth falls open in surprise.

"But Caroline..."

"I'm sure she has her reasons for running away." Sheena sighs, then turns to Anna. "But you don't need to worry. I'm still here. And I'm going to make sure everything turns out perfectly from now on." She steers them both back towards the table. "Alright, everyone. Where did we get to? Speeches? Matt, you're up."

"You were right when you said nothing fazes her," TJ mutters, his mouth inches from my ear. "But what was all that with Caroline?"

"We need to go get Sheriff Foster," I say, tugging on TJ's hand and slipping quietly towards the door. We get almost all the way there before Pamela waves me over.

"Ronnie, dear, what happened with poor Caroline? I've been so worried about her. She hasn't seemed at all like herself lately. You're friends with her, aren't you? Go and check on her, will you?"

I promise to make sure her niece is ok, even though my stomach turns over at the thought of the giant lie I'm telling. The woman in front of me pats me warmly on the cheek, then turns back to listen to Matt's awkward, self-deprecating speech. I stare at him for a moment, but either he doesn't notice me or he's deliberately keeping his gaze averted. Either way, I feel the sting of being ignored - again - by one of my oldest friends and fight the tears that prick at the edge of my eyes.

"Come on," I say to TJ, who's watching me a lot more carefully than I realized. "We really need to see the sheriff."

TJ obediently leaves the diner with me, but we only make it half a dozen steps before we see the figure of Caroline hunched over on a bench. TJ drifts towards her, but I'm quick to lay a restraining hand on his arm. It doesn't matter. Caroline spots us long before we reach her.

"Was it you?" Her voice is laden with such bitter anger that it stops me in my tracks. *Was what me?*

Caroline points towards the diner.

"I suppose Matt told you, did he? And you couldn't resist running here to ruin everything. It would have all been alright if you'd just kept our secret. It never should have happened. I wish it hadn't! But I got your messages, ok? I did everything you asked me to. I paid you all the money I have! I thought that would be enough."

She's babbling incoherently now and I look at TJ who's just as confused as I am. The only person who can explain what's going on is Caroline, but she's starting to pace now, looking more and more unhinged with every step she takes.

"I got your first message and I thought it was some kind of a joke. Oh, ha ha, let's prank Caroline about the thing she's already feeling guilty about. I ignored it. But then you messaged again. And then when you asked for money..." She shakes her head. "It's not like I have a lot of it lying around, you know! And even when I paid you it wasn't enough. I thought if I could just get through the next few hours...through the wedding..."

"Caroline..." I pull out my phone, tapping through to my message bank before angling it towards her. "I haven't been messaging you. I don't think I've ever messaged you!" I slide my thumb over my contacts and nod to myself. "I don't even have your number."

"Let me see that!" Quick as a cat, Caroline snatches my phone and scrolls through my messages, her eyes greedily taking in every message I've sent and received over the last few days. She frowns, shaking her head with every word she reads.

"You must have another phone. What do they call it on TV? A burner." She nods. "That'd be right. An anonymous phone to go with your anonymous threats and demands."

"Who's been threatening you?" TJ asks.

"If it's about what happened," I say, thinking sadly of Amy's poor, broken body. "I'm sure people will understand. You had your reasons. Or maybe you just snapped. Who hasn't lashed out in a fit of anger, and -"

"What are you talking about?" Caroline thrusts my phone back at me. "Lashed out? What do you mean?"

"Amy Callaghan. You - hurt her." I fumble the word *murder* at the last moment. Right now, looking at tiny, skinny little Caroline I can't imagine her murdering anyone, and I shiver at the thought of what must have powered her to snatch up a rolling pin and...

"No, I didn't!" Caroline's face pales. "I didn't do anything to Amy!"

"Then what were you talking about just now?" I'm genuinely confused. "What were you feeling guilty about? What did you do that was so terrible?"

"I..." Caroline whips her head away from me, her eyes closing as if she's too miserable to speak the words in front of a watching audience, even if it's just me and TJ. "I kissed Matt."

Chapter Eleven

"Ok. Let's go back to the beginning."

Sheriff Foster sounds weary and to be honest I can't blame him. We've been sitting at his desk for a few minutes now and talking mostly in circles. When I told Caroline we ought to go to the sheriff's station to report what had been happening she gave me a look like a deer in headlights and asked me, without a hint of sarcasm, whether I thought she was going to go to jail for kissing her best friend's fiancé.

"I kissed Matt." It's almost as if repeatedly saying her dark secret out loud has stripped it of all the power it had over her. Caroline seems lighter, somehow, as if a heavy weight is finally lifting off her narrow shoulders, which I guess in some ways it is.

"And this is relevant to my investigation because...?" The sheriff gazes past Caroline to me, and when she turns her head quizzically towards me too I realize I'm going to have to do my best to explain why I had the brilliant idea of coming here to begin with.

"Caroline has been being blackmailed. Somebody found out her secret - about this apparent kiss between her and Matt - and has been threatening her."

This makes the sheriff sit up, and I prompt Caroline to show him the messages on her phone. She purses her lips, then taps through to reach the litany of cruel threats she's been receiving for days now. She angles the screen so the sheriff can read them, and I watch his eyebrows raise.

"And do you have any idea who sent these messages, Ms. Mackie? Who has been threatening you?"

"Blackmailing. Asking for money." I take the phone and scroll back to the messages that demanded payment and show them to him. "That's a crime, right? Extortion."

The sheriff makes a note but his expression remains unreadable. He turns back to Caroline.

"You still have no idea who's behind this?"

Caroline shakes her head, biting her lip anxiously.

"I mean, I thought it might be Amy, but then..."

"Did you confront her?"

I can practically see the cogs whirring in Sheriff Foster's brain and I know exactly where he's going with this.

"I asked her," Caroline began. "But she didn't seem to know what I was talking about." Her lower lip juts out. "She was kind of mean. Asked why she would ever bother messaging me about anything at all, and..."

"This was before the murder," I clarify, worried my clueless friend is about to incriminate herself which is so not what I intended when I suggested we come to the station tonight and make a report. "Right?"

Caroline catches my look and nods in a way that makes the sheriff's eyes narrow.

"Ms. Swan, perhaps it's best if you wait outside while I..."

"Do you think the person who threatened me is the same person who killed Amy?" Caroline's eyes widen like saucers, and I direct Sheriff Foster's attention back to her and the case at hand, and away from any suspicion of me leading the witness. *Someone has to lead her, or none of this would ever have even come to light.*

"Ms. Mackie." He draws a breath. "How long had the, ah, relationship between you and Matt been going on?"

Caroline blinks in confusion.

"The what?"

"How long had the two of you been involved?"

"I've known him forever." Caroline tilts her head to one side. "Since high school, at least. Maybe longer. You know what Westhaven's like. Everyone's known everyone since they were in diapers." She catches her breath, remembering that Seth Foster hasn't known anyone in town that long. "Well, I mean...almost everyone."

"I think what Sheriff Foster wants to know," I put in, trying to keep Caroline from getting too distracted, and trying to keep Seth from losing his mind. "Is how long you two have been...together." I raise my eyebrows. "You know. *Together.*"

"Oh!" Caroline colors, then - no, I don't imagine it - she actually cringes. "We aren't together! It was just this one time." She swallows, looking as if she is being forced to tell the worst secret she has. Which I guess she is. "It was under the mistletoe. You know? That big sprig of it that sits over the door to the diner? We got caught beneath it, and so we kissed, and...someone must have seen us."

Silence settles over the room and I feel like my sense of disbelief must be shared by the sheriff, even though he has a better poker face than I do.

"That's it?"

"Ms. Mackie." Sheriff Foster's features crinkle into a frown and I see now that he's struggling not to laugh. "Are you telling me that this all started after one kiss under the mistletoe?"

Caroline nods her head firmly, and I have to fight the urge to put my arms around her.

"You do realize that Matt has probably kissed every girl in Westhaven under that particular mistletoe bough?"

I feel the sheriff's curious gaze turn on me and stumble over my words.

"It's just a bit of silly festive fun. It won't have meant anything to him at all."

"It certainly didn't mean anything to me!" Caroline protests. "Except that I felt so guilty for what we did to Anna. And then when the messages started..."

"When did they start?" I ask. "After Amy came to town?"

"Before." Caroline shakes her head. "It's why I felt sort of relieved when Anna promoted her to maid of honor instead of me. It was only right." She pauses. "And when she died, when Anna asked me to take on the job I was determined that everything was going to work out just perfectly for her. To make up for kissing her fiancé like that." She pauses. "And to make up for what happened to Amy, of course."

"I think it's unlikely the two cases are related," Sheriff Foster says, after a long moment while he struggles to regain his composure. "Although of course we take the blackmail and extortion seriously. I can't see how there is anything connecting it to Ms. Callaghan's murder. Especially not if the messages began before she even came to town."

"And you already caught the guy who hurt her, didn't you?" I prompt, eager to pin the blame back on Liam Wright now I know the real reason for Caroline's strange behavior. I feel a prickle of shame for ever thinking the young woman next to me could be capable of committing a murder.

"Ah, no." Sheriff Foster folds his hands and peers over them at me, looking a little unsettled. "It turned out he had an alibi. A pretty compelling one."

"Then who killed Amy?"

The door to the sheriff's station flies open and Deputy Dell bursts in, still clad in all her finery from the rehearsal dinner. She halts, taking in Caroline, me, and the sheriff in one swift glance. She scowls, looking surprised and annoyed to see us sitting with her boss.

"What's going on?"

"Just a small matter, Deputy. Nothing you need to worry about. Especially not this evening." Seth smiles indulgently at his colleague. "I know how important this rehearsal dinner is to you."

"Yes." Sheena smiles, and for a moment I fancy I see a glimmer of triumph in the eyes that sweep over Caroline once more. "Anna has asked me to step in and be her maid of honor. I'm sure you understand, Caroline. After everything..."

Caroline pales but nods her head. She evidently doesn't trust herself to speak but starts chewing on a thumbnail. I feel a strange flicker of sympathy and put an arm around her.

"That was all just a misunderstanding. Come on, Caroline. We'll go back there right now and explain everything."

"But you can't!" Sheena shrieks. We all stare at her and she lets out an awkward giggle, before patting her bouffant hair neatly into place. "I mean, you're too late. The party's all breaking up and everyone is heading home. Anna told me to tell you goodnight, and she'll see you at the church tomorrow." She turns to Caroline. "She's willing to let you remain as her backup bridesmaid if you'd like, but we'll all understand if you'd rather just skip the whole wedding."

My grip on Caroline's shoulders tightens and I shoot a level glare in Sheena's direction.

"She'll be there. We all will." I smile. "Wouldn't miss it for the world."

"Did you need something else, Sheena?" Sheriff Foster glances at us and clears his throat, shooting for professionalism. "Ah, Deputy Dell?"

Sheena's scowl has deepened and she opens her mouth to say more, but before she can, she spots a familiar black leather something resting on the corner of the sheriff's desk.

"My purse!"

"Right!" Sheriff Foster shakes his head. "I'm sorry. I noticed you left it here, and I was going to bring it over to you at the church, when..." He sounds a lot more flustered than he needs to be, and I fight a flicker of amusement at seeing the usually composed sheriff stumble over his words. "Here." He stands up and passes the bag across us to Sheena, who snatches it from him with an ungracious smile.

"It is a lovely purse," Caroline sighs, as her gaze follows the exchange. "I remember Anna used to have one just like it."

"Did she?"

There's something strange about Sheena's voice, and I sense the sheriff's posture change, suggesting I'm not the only one to notice it.

"Well, I guess she is the kind of person to set the fashion around here in Westhaven." Sheena giggles, one hand straying to her collarbone where she's wearing an elegant, vintage-looking locket fastened on a ribbon around her neck.

"Where did you get that?" I get out of my seat, angling my head to get a better look at the locket. There's something familiar about it I can't quite place. "I think I've seen it before."

"You haven't." Sheena scrambles back, away from me, and doesn't look where she's going. She collides painfully with the edge of a table and sprawls forward, her hands losing their hold on her purse, which lands upside down on the ground, spilling its contents in a wide arc.

"Here," I say, dropping to my knees to gather Sheena's lost belongings. "Let me help you."

"No! Don't!"

My hand passes over one phone, and then another, and as I lift them both I frown, surveying each one in turn.

"That's my work phone," Sheena says, snatching one off me. "A lot of people have a separate phone, you know."

"Right." I smile but as I pile the rest of Sheena's belongings back into her bag one of the scraps of paper I see on the ground makes me stop. I bend down and stare at it, trying to make sense of the torn piece of badly-printed text. *Congratulations on winning...* I slide it free from the pile and make out a couple more key words. *Cruise. Bahamas.* "Did you print this out?" I hold the scrap towards the light and am surprised when Sheriff Foster lifts it out of my hands.

"This is the workroom printer, isn't it? I recognize that red line down the middle. I've been on at Joe to get that fixed, but..."

I barely hear him. My brain is too busy connecting the pieces of a puzzle I finally see laid out in front of me, like scraps of paper on the ground. Like a second phone. Like a necklace I last saw around the neck of a dead girl...

"*You* killed Amy Callaghan."

"What?" Sheena lets out an awkward, high-pitched laugh. "What are you talking about?"

"You sent Bella away on a cruise so that she wouldn't be around to be Anna's maid of honor. And then when Amy came along, you got rid of her too…" I glance at Caroline. "And you intimidated Caroline with messages about her secret…"

"I didn't!"

"Caroline." I hold out my hand to my friend, who is watching this interaction in a sort of wide-eyed stupor. "Give me your phone." Dumbly, she hands it over, and we all watch as I hit the call button, ringing the sender of all those mean messages. A factory-set ringtone goes off from the phone Sheena holds clutched tightly in one of her hands, announcing her guilt to the whole room.

"Deputy…"

Sheriff Foster's voice is all it takes to shock Sheena back into action, and she throws the phone in my direction, distracting me just enough to buy her time to fly back through the door and out into the waiting room. What she's forgotten, though, what we've all forgotten, is that TJ is waiting right there. He hasn't heard our whole discussion, but he knows a guilty person when he sees one, and he uses his body to block the exit, just long enough for Sheriff Foster to lunge past me and out into the waiting area, to secure his suspect.

Chapter Twelve

"So it was Sheena all along? She's responsible for everything?"

"It looks that way. She isn't even denying it now, although it took being confronted with the evidence to make her come clean. It seems so obvious now, but she was pretty good at covering her tracks."

"Of course. And she was involved in the investigation right from the start..." TJ shakes his head. "I hate to think how far she would have gone to keep herself free of suspicion. She would have framed an innocent person for murder."

"Well, she had the perfect fall guy in Liam.

TJ and I are talking in whispers as we sit in the waiting area of the sheriff's station. Caroline is leaning against me, her head on my shoulder. Her low, measured breathing makes me think she's fallen asleep, which is a miracle in its own right, until the door swings open and a second unbelievable thing happens.

"Is it true?"

Anna Chambers bursts into the room, sees Caroline, and drops her voice to a whisper. Her eyes are on me, fierce and intense.

"Did Sheena kill Amy?"

I nod, which makes Caroline stir, and I slowly maneuver around until she's leaning on the arm of the chair, not me, allowing me to get to my feet and cross the room to where Anna is standing. She looks so pale and unsteady on her feet that I reach out my arms to her and fold her into the most unlikely, awkward hug in the history of hugging.

"I can't believe it," she murmurs into my shoulder. "She killed Amy. And she was trying to make me believe Caroline had something to do with it."

Caroline lets out a low snore and we both seem to find this funny. At once, the idea that innocent, idiotic Caroline could be responsible for a murder is proved to be utterly ridiculous. Anna straightens and we both smile in spite of ourselves.

"She was threatening Caroline," I say. "Extorting money, blackmailing her over...something that happened a little while ago." I shrug my shoulders. Just because Anna deserves to know what Sheena did, doesn't mean everyone's secrets should come out.

The door to the sheriff's station opens and Matt cautiously steps inside, doing a wary double-take when he sees me and his fiancée standing so close together and looking, for maybe the first time ever, like we don't want to kill each other. He shoots me a grateful smile and skirts past us to join TJ on an empty chair across the room.

"It seems as if she was responsible for getting Bella out of town too," I continue, wanting Anna to understand just what has been going on over the last few days and weeks. "It seems like she thought if she got rid of Bella and Caroline you'd welcome her as your stand-in maid of honor. She's been in awe of you for years."

Anna shudders.

"And that's almost exactly what I did do! After Amy..." She sniffs. "After Amy..."

"I don't think she meant to kill Amy," I say, trying to be as generous as I can with my words. "At least, I don't think that was her goal at the start. I think she just wanted to scare her off, maybe persuade her to leave town again. When that didn't work, it sounds as if she just picked up whatever weapon was closest to hand, and..."

Anna's face pales again and as she rubs at her eyes with the cuff of her sweater I catch the way her engagement ring glints in the light.

"I don't even know if I should get married now." Anna twists the ring awkwardly on her finger. "It feels like the whole thing is cursed. If Sheena was willing to do all that she did just to get to be a part of it...what does that say about Matt and I? About me?"

I take a long, slow breath in. I can hardly believe I'm about to say what I'm about to say, but I also know there's no other advice I can offer. I have been more opposed to this match than anyone, and maybe that makes me just the right person to keep it together.

"I think you have to remember why the two of you want to get married in the first place. You love each other, right?"

Anna glances across the room to where Matt and TJ are having an awkward, whispered conversation and even I can't mistake the love in her gaze. I'm surprised I never noticed it before now, but then I never spent a lot of time looking at Anna Chambers in the past. I tended to avoid acknowledging her at all. *They really do care about each other. And even though I hate to say it, they seem...happy!* Matt lifts his head and catches Anna's eye and I feel like I'm witnessing a moment meant just for the two of them. I drop my gaze. I've been against this marriage from the start, but that certainly doesn't mean it ever occurred to me to sabotage it. Sheena did everything she could to destroy things to serve her own ends - to get close to Anna

Chambers and force the kind of friendship she dreamt of having with the former queen of our high school. Am I guilty of trying to hang on equally tightly to Matt when I really need to let him go?

I wouldn't have gone to the lengths Sheena went to, I tell myself, but it's not much comfort. I wouldn't have killed anyone, and I wouldn't have threatened and manipulated people out of the way to get to *Anna Chambers,* but I certainly wasn't as supportive of Matt as I could have been. I've been clinging so hard to how I remember us being in the past that I haven't bothered to acknowledge who he's become in the present, and who he's choosing to build his life with in the future.

"You know, Anna…"

"I'm not going to ask you to be my bridesmaid."

And just like that, Anna Chambers is her old self again. I take a step backward and she straightens up to her full height, looking me dead in the eyes as she folds her arms across her front. There's a challenge in her gaze and I feel like some of her inner fire sparks back into life.

"Maybe I don't need any bridesmaids at all."

Caroline starts to stir, and Anna softens, just a fraction, so that if I wasn't standing this close to her I never would have noticed it.

"I think maybe one will be more than enough. Caroline will be just the bridesmaid you need."

"Bridesmaid?" Anna smiles, but she's already moving away from me, towards her friend who is properly awake now, and anxious about this particular reunion. "Caroline's not just a bridesmaid. She's the best friend I've got, and she's going to be my maid of honor." She slides into the chair next to Caroline, looking serious. "If she still wants to be."

Caroline hesitates for half a second, then smiles, and it's as if all the stress and worry of the last few days never even happened.

"Of course I do! Best friends forever?"

Anna slips her arm through Caroline's and smiles at her as if there's nobody else in the room.

"Best friends forever."

I roll my eyes and turn away, unable to completely hide my smile. Anna Chambers as a best friend? Caroline is welcome to her. But maybe I can learn to tolerate her a little better, for Matt's sake, if nothing else.

• • • •

SHERIFF FOSTER LOOKS utterly exhausted when he finally comes out to send the last of us lingering witnesses home. And by *us,* I literally mean *us two*. Caroline, Anna, and Matt are long gone by the time the sheriff comes out to close up the station, and he looks surprised to find anyone still here at all.

"Ms. Swan." He recovers himself quickly, acknowledging TJ with a nod. "Still hanging around here, I see. Don't you have anywhere better to spend your evening than the waiting area of the Westhaven sheriff's station?"

"I take it Sheena co-operated? She told you everything?"

Sheriff Foster's eyebrows lift but he smiles, and I can hear the teasing lilt in his voice even if TJ can't.

"You know I can't discuss an active investigation with you."

"Even when I helped you catch the killer?"

His eyes sparkle but he isn't giving an inch. But then, neither am I.

"That locket she was wearing belonged to Amy. Did she tell you that? I bet it'll be a match to the broken chain links you found at the crime scene."

"Goodnight, Ms. Swan."

"And what about those messages she was sending to Caroline? That has to count for something. And the flyer she printed out about the competition prize win. She bought those tickets for Bella Villodan, didn't she? She invented that whole competition winner thing as a way to get her out of town over Christmas."

"Goodnight, Ms. Swan." The sheriff pushes the door to the street open and holds it there until we take the hint, and in the end, TJ is the one who leads us out into the night.

"You have to admit that without my help..."

"Without your help, this case would have taken a lot longer to solve," Seth acknowledges as I pass through the door. "You should consider a career in law enforcement." He glances over his shoulder, even though he must know the station is empty except for him. When he speaks it's in a low voice, little more than a whisper, and this time I can't tell if he's teasing me or not. "There may even be a vacancy for a new deputy before too much longer. You know. In case you were looking for a career change." He winks, so quickly I'm not sure I didn't imagine it. "Just something to think about, if you ever get bored of pulling extra shifts at the Slice."

I'm so stunned it takes me a minute to think up any kind of a response, and that minute is all Seth needs to pull the door closed, trapping me on the outside of it. He switches the lights off just for good measure, plunging the station into darkness and saying more eloquently than words could that he is done for the night.

"Well, that was an eventful evening," TJ says, steering me away from the sheriff's station and along the street to where he left his car what seems like a lifetime ago. "Did you tell your dad what was going on?"

My blood flashes cold in my veins and I reach for my phone, frantically jabbing at it until I pull up a string of messages. I slide down to the most recent and let out a sigh of relief as I read it.

TJ filled me in on what's going on. You take care, kiddo.

I turn to smile at TJ and realize he's watching me kind of warily as if he's worried I might think he overstepped by contacting Dad on my behalf.

"Thanks for letting him know. He would have worried."

"I figured." TJ slings a companionable arm around my shoulders and I lean into it, grateful that he is there, and thinking that if he hadn't been, Sheena might just have escaped the sheriff's station this evening and caused untold mayhem in her desire to avoid getting arrested. Things could have ended so badly. I shiver, and TJ hugs me closer.

"So, about this new hobby of yours..."

I angle my head so I can look at him.

"Solving crime."

"What about it?"

"You're pretty good at it. Ever thought of making a career out of it?"

I wonder how close TJ had been standing to me when Sheriff Foster made the very same suggestion.

"You mean..."

"Become a private investigator. I know the chances are you'd just end up trying to catch cheating boyfriends and missing pets more than actual cold-blooded killers, but I bet you'd still find plenty of work." He grins at me. "You know what Westhaven's like. An absolute hotbed of crime and injustice."

"And you think being a private investigator would help fix that?"

TJ shrugs.

"It couldn't hurt. You'd get to be completely independent and only take on the cases you think are important. You could do some real good in the town, Ronnie. Actually help people. You did say you were trying to figure out what to do with yourself now you're staying in town. Or do you want to stay working at the Slice until you're old and gray?"

"No," I admit, thinking that no matter how fun the last few weeks have been, I certainly won't miss hanging up my apron for the final time - again. I've been on the lookout for an opportunity, for something in all of Westhaven that I would like to spend my life doing. Maybe that opportunity has been staring me in the face all this time, and I just never realized it until now. "I'll think about it," I promise TJ, as we make our way slowly back to where he parked his car. *Private Investigator Veronica Swan, at your service!* It's certainly worth considering...

Epilogue

"**I** now pronounce you husband and wife. You may now..."

A cheer goes up through the gathered congregation so nobody even gets to hear Pastor Brooke say the immortal words *kiss the bride*, but it doesn't matter because Matt sweeps Anna off her feet all the same, which makes everyone cheer all the louder.

Yes, even me. What can I say, I'm a sucker for a happy ending.

"All ok, Ronnie?" Dad asks, as I stealthily wipe at a tear. I nod and return his smile as he reaches for his handkerchief. "Yeah, I guess a wedding is enough to make even the most cynical of us a little misty-eyed..."

I slip my arm through Dad's and we gradually get to our feet, ready to follow the rest of the congregation through the church doors and outside to celebrate with the new Mr.and Mrs.Taylor. I don't think I've ever seen either Matt or Anna this happy, and I think about how many unexpected last-minute obstacles they had to overcome to get to this point. *I suppose I can be happy for them too*, I think, letting go of the last bit of resentment I've held onto about this match, and this marriage. I might not have picked these particular two people to wind up together, but they chose each other and it looks like they're happy with their decision. *I think they're going to work out ok.*

"Excuse me a second, kiddo!" I feel Dad slip free from my grasp and watch as he spots Pamela Kaufman across the aisle. He's remarkably spry, for a man who's still slowly recovering from a heart attack, and I pull a face as he bows and chivalrously offers his arm to her instead.

"They make a good-looking couple, don't they?"

The sly voice of Sheriff Foster makes me turn, and I'm surprised to see the *good-looking couple* he's referring to isn't Matt and Anna, but my dad and Pamela.

"So when is the next Westhaven wedding going to be? Do you have your dress all picked out, as the daughter of the groom-to-be?"

"Hush!" I glance over my shoulder to check his words haven't carried. "Dad and Pamela are just good friends."

"Uh-huh." He's smiling and I fight the urge to laugh. I haven't bought that line for weeks now and it looks like Dad and Pamela aren't fooling anyone else about their burgeoning relationship, either.

Seth and I fall into step as we make our way slowly out of the church and end up standing together in the bustling churchyard as people pose for pictures and compliment the newlyweds on a wonderful service and the happy life they have to look forward to together.

"Well, it looks like everyone made it through the wedding unscathed." Seth brushes a stray piece of confetti from the shoulder of his navy suit with a grin. "Mostly."

"Hey, new suit! You aren't dressed all in black, for once."

His grin widens.

"Well, you see, I had it on good authority that people who dress all in black are suspicious, and..."

"Ronnie!"

We both look up as TJ hurries towards us, fumbling with his tie and finger-combing his hair into place.

"I made it." He smiles breathlessly at me as he falls into place beside me and Seth. "I know I missed the ceremony but I got here just in time for the reception, and that has to count for something, doesn't it?"

"What are you doing here? I thought you had to work!"

"Ah, yeah." The slightest hint of color appears on TJ's cheeks. "I called in just about every favor I'm owed, near enough sold my soul for the next six months, but it worked out in the end." He draws himself up to his full height, then bows. "May I present to you: your gift."

I'm confused, and he grins at me.

"I know how much you were dreading going to this reception on your own, so here I am, your very own Christmas present. A plus one, a bodyguard, a companion to help you survive the wedding reception you've been dreading all winter. How about it, are you ready to face the lions together?" He offers me his arm and I take it, glancing over my shoulder at Seth who salutes us both and takes a step back. I wonder for a second if I see disappointment flicker across his face like a shadow, but he's smiling again as he turns to find someone else to talk to and I'm sure I imagined it. TJ and I fall in step with our neighbors, joining the rest of the crowd as it makes its way towards the reception hall, ready to continue the celebrations.

It wasn't like I wanted to spend the rest of the day on my own, but finding myself on TJ's arm, when I'd convinced myself that wasn't going to happen, is a little bit of a surprise.

"I know this is no prom photo," TJ remarks in a whisper, as we wave to Dad and Pamela and join the rest of the milling wedding guests. "But I hope it isn't too much of a disappointing gift. And I know I'm a day early, but we won't get the chance to say it on the actual holiday itself, so this is as good a time as any. Merry Christmas, Veronica. I hope the new year brings you everything you wish for."

My gaze meets my TJ's and my heart lifts, swelling with gratitude for my friends, for my town, for the whole new life I have just over the horizon.

"Merry Christmas," I say, whispering the words to all of Westhaven, and most of all to myself. "And a Happy New Year!

• • • •

The End

About the Author

When Rachel Beattie isn't writing stories, she's usually reading them - especially of the cozy mystery variety. A lifelong devotee of Agatha Christie, she loves putting ze little grey cells to work and is especially fond of anything that can make her laugh while she's collecting a clue or two.

• • • •

Join her mailing list[1] for more information, new release news, exclusives and bonus content.

---

1. https://mailchi.mp/003ddbbcc668/newsletter-subscribers

Also by Rachel Beattie

A Serenity Suites Cozy Mystery
Cassie Clinton and the First Fatality
Double Trouble for Cassie Clinton
Cassie Clinton and the Triple Threat

A Slice of Life Cozy Mystery
Love, Lies and Pumpkin Spice
Wed, Dead and Gingerbread
Crime Scenes and Blackcurrant Cream
Spirits, Spells and Caramel
Broken Hearts and Strawberry Tarts
Black Tie and Vanilla Pie
A Slice of Life Cozy Mystery Books 1-3

A Very Merry Murder Mystery
The Santa Slaughter
The First Date Disaster
The Body in the Bookstore

The Harmony Inn Homicide
The Scandal at the Spa
The Babysitter Bungle
The Campground Killer
The Deadly Dinner Party
The Flower Shop Felony
A Very Merry Murder Mystery Books 1-3

www.ingramcontent.com/pod-product-compliance
Lightning Source LLC
Chambersburg PA
CBHW022146150726
47992CB00002B/788